The Oosik

Scott Nitzel

SCOTT
NITZEL

The Oosik

Library of Congress Control Number: 2021923411

ISBN 979-8-9853210-0-5   SOFT COVER $19.95 USA
ISBN 979-8-9853210-1-2   EPUB $4.95 USA

To my mother, Margy Fay

The Oosik

An ancient walrus encapsulated in glacial ice from twelve thousand years ago was slowly mashed against rock and debris until the thawing ice age allowed his emergence to be found by mankind, who in return chiseled and cut and tugged until his long boney Oosik was ripped away from his carcass.

Long after the remnants of that walrus had descended to the depths of the Bering Sea, its Oosik will remain a travel-partner with humans, who will use its considerable weight as a bludgeoning club on a noisy or struggling seal that's interrupting their larger hunt.

This Oosik of study is a meter in length, thicker than a baseball bat's handle, sleek and smooth with a creamy eggshell color base with swirls of caramelized deep orange, translucent red ocher stains, and rich brown hues from absorption of minerals over thousands of years while polishing to a vibrant and attractive sight, which will remain a shiny relic of desire while in custody for centuries to follow.

My research of the Oosik had launched an earnest leap forward while camping along the estuary shore outside Unalakleet, Alaska. On that day I was wrapping up my second colloquy with the local Inuit ceremonial director, a man named Aput, and with campfire burning and a summer starry night to gather folklore of this Oosik, a bottle of Pinot Grigio was shared amongst us. I would that evening celebrate my agreement to research this relic in further detail, this Oosik; this penis bone from the gigantic, and long ago extinct Artic Walrus. Oosik is the name for penis bone used by the local Inuit. For two days I had sessions with Aput as he fervently presided over conversations of his knowledge to this Oosik. I was treated to singing and dance and further stories concerning Inuits and their descendants. I was also advised that my temporary campsite was located in close proximity to where several events relative to the Oosik had taken place.

As for my purpose in this endeavor, normally I would freelance this assignment through the *Journal of American Rare Objects, JARO*; however, it would be unjust to limit this adventurous story of the Oosik to their esoteric subscribers as it warrants the broadest readership, so before returning to my home in northern California, I stayed behind to meander the known trail as it first appeared to the adopted Oosik.

In the morning I did strike camp and traveled five hours north to Kotzebue to survey another marker significant to the Oosik, but to round out my last hour with Aput, I chose to launch the conversation towards my beliefs that burial coffins should be used like time capsules that are stuffed with personal sacred objects, and that I wanted several of my grave goods stored around and on top of my corpse, as much as can fit and to include my journals and paintings. I went on to explain to Aput that I wanted any future archeological dig on my burial site to easily tell them just who the hell I was. Aput described the dichotomy of his Inuit-Eskimo-Native American customs that before the arrival of Christians in the 1880's that dead bodies were placed on a hilltop to purposely be devoured by wolves.

The earliest known records of the Oosik, as chronicled to me by the local historian Hughie Miller who works from the Arctic Heritage Center in Kotzebue, is that it was first in the hands of the Alornerk family-tribe and it was passed down through generations spanning just over three centuries while they inhabited a nearby and ancient tribal area, which today is an underwater forest. I was alongside the pebbly seashore while Hughie described the frequent warring between Inuit communities over territorial disputes, but somehow through unrecorded tactics the Oosik would remain stowed with its inherited handlers and not captured by another tribal leader, not yet anyways. I gazed out over the Bering Sea trying to image the importance to a section of tribal ground that's now submerged under the ocean as a result of the ice age melting away and raising the sea level.

The Oosik was eventually confiscated by a larger concurring community of Inuits and consequently it was handed to Natan, their leader, where it lived inside his teepee-shaped tent and also went under its first alteration when that tribes artisan, who was the best craftsman amongst the regional tribes, went to work carving an oval shaped Brown Owl just off center of the bone onto a concave smooth surface section which looked like someone's thumb had compressed into the Oosik spreading it out wider than any other area. The elliptical shaped Brown Owl was spoken among the group as his greatest etching, and it aroused Natan that the Oosik needed more design work, so it was decided that his artisan would use a section between the Brown Owl and the tip of the Oosik to engrave a female face with antlers, which to them was Pukimna, the mother and goddess overseeing the reincarnation of revered walrus and caribou. The Oosik was now a spiritual relic.

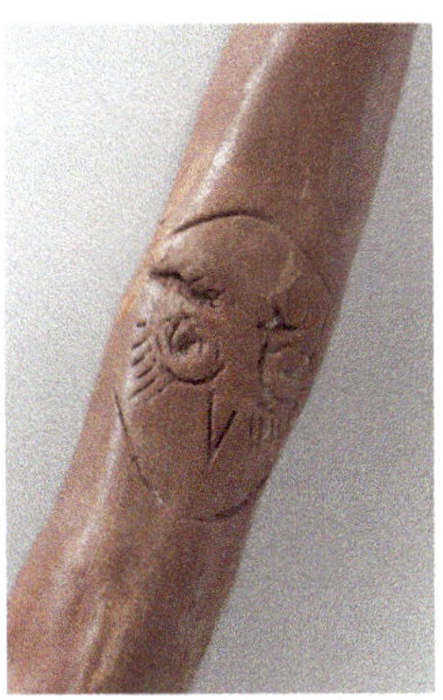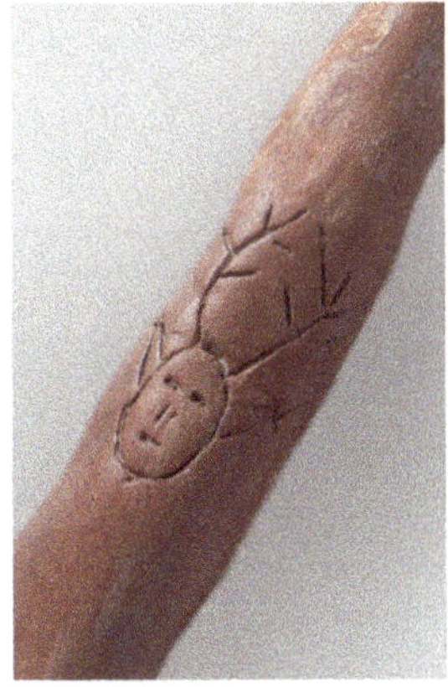

I followed the trail south for four hours to the site of this recorded event, the first trade of the Oosik, near the shores of Golovin on the Norton Sound of western Alaska, where in 1870 a powerful storyteller named Ujurak had ascended to shaman of his tribe at an early age, and he was in possession of his deceased brother's private maps detailing routes to better hunting areas, and to include knowledge of coastlines and distances, which the decedents of Natan could put to great use and offered to take the maps in exchange for the Oosik.

My newest study area revealed that Ujurak's deceased brother had been a detailed and proficient cartographer both throughout the regional islands as well as inland, and his work compiled of nineteen accurate sketches. The decedents of the once flourishing tribe of Natan had waned in size due to disease and lost battles and their hopes were that these newly acquired charts would quickly help restock their food supplies.

Ujurak the shaman, the new owner of the Oosik, was not only healer of the spirit world but also the tribe astrologer. He used his ceremonies to speak of the thirty-three stars know to him, six of which he had names for, and most profound was his teachings to the thirteen months in his lunar calendar. Ujurak himself carved thirteen equal and parallel notches each two finger widths apart into the Oosik. The Oosik was now his navigational tool to measure stars and calculate distances.

For ten years Ujurak the shaman would lay the Oosik in his lap while sharing the teachings of the spirit world and how it connected with the natural world, but these teachings were nearing the end as soon as the Presbyterians arrived. The new missionaries preached the gospel and intensely began to pressure Ujurak to covert.

The three daughters of Ujurak did not desire to be uplifted from barbarism into Christianity and certainly they did not want to coalesce with a formal school as suggested by the newcomers. The oldest daughter was set to marry into a different tribe and was excited to change her protocol and dress, and Ujurak being so savvy and wanting peace, knew that sharing his daughter with another tribe would provide him guarantees. Ujurak had a choice as it concerned his daughters: give the oldest to marry or relinquish to the Presbyterian demands.

I traveled by speedboat two hours south through Norton Sound returning to Unalakleet where preserved and on display inside a back room under secured glass inside the original First Presbyterian church, although now renovated to museum, is the long seal skin pouch which once secured the Oosik while the three daughters departed by themselves carrying the relic on their way to join the Christians. For much of three days they paddled their skin boat while eating smoked King salmon belly and Moose Sticks: smoked moose sausage commonly eaten during a hunt as animals won't hear chewing. The imprints and stitching on the pouch show an image of three girls inside a skin boat running their fingers through what must have been calm waters.

Known area of the Oosik to this point

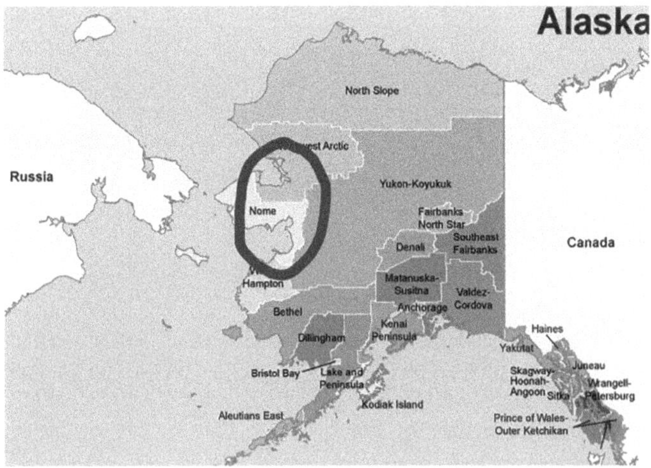

The Oosik became exclusive property to youngest of the three daughters, Tanaraq, who was only twelve during her arrival with the Christian missionaries.

Of the three sisters, it was Tanaraq who had the deepest connection with the Oosik and she boasted to others about the strength and the protection from evil that the Oosik provided her, and she enjoyed carrying the Oosik with her to school as it was a piece of conversation while others gravitated towards the new object, which afforded her a sense of acceptance when others needed to touch it.

While Tanaraq was an outgoing and enthusiastic fifteen years old, and with three years of formal English lessons, she entered this poem about the Oosik into her school notebook, which she said was inspired by her father's final instruction before leaving home, "Don't trade it for coin."

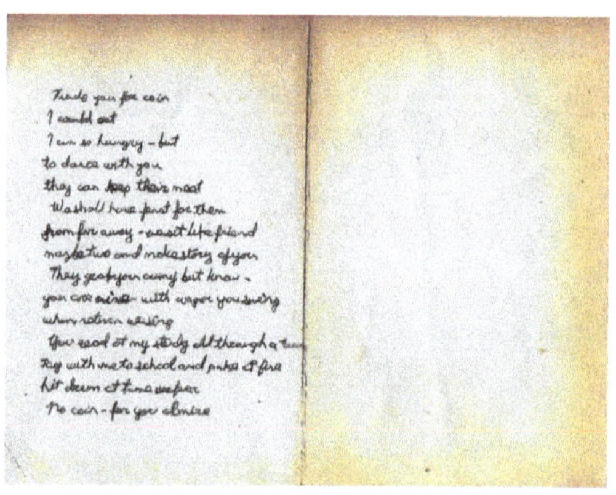

Trade you for coin
I could eat
I am so hungry - but
to dance with you
they can keep their meat
We shall have feast for them
from far away - we sit like friend
maybe two and make story of you
They grab you away but know -
you are mine - with anger you swing
when return we sing
You read at my study all through a tear
tag with me to school and poke at fire
hit drum at time we fear
No coin - for you admire

Tanaraq's poem was the first mention of the Oosik using English words, and I was permitted to take this picture from her school notebook, which is also on display in the same room as is the long seal skin pouch.

The Oosik remained with Tanaraq throughout her young adulthood while she enjoyed prayer, scoffed at the mention of polygamy, and became one of the first Inuits to marry in a Christian Church. She prized the Oosik until the death of her father, Ujurak, who himself converted to Christianity and is buried in a cemetery, like a westerner, on the outskirts of Unalakleet. Following his burial, the Oosik was handed down to her son, Cupun, who took the English surname Nash. The accounts of Tanaraq were known as a gregarious young woman that would sit with her friends in circle and make games and stories of the Oosik and prepare for some future festival when folks would travel from far away to attend their summer solstice party of fermented beverage with dance and feast honoring the Oosik.

The event that dislodged the Oosik from generations of native reverence happened on a summer day while Cupun was dredging for gold with his daughter and two others along the Yukon River not three miles from his home in St. Michael, Alaska. Cupun and his longtime friend were igniting dynamite that they had placed into crevasses of bedrock in hopes of loosening and exposing a vein of gold flakes or perhaps a nugget. It was to be a weekend camping trip in the wilderness with their teenage children, but became so much more when the shallow waters glistened with prosperity. Throughout that afternoon they roasted wild bird over the open fire but without once pausing to enjoy a peaceful meal as the constant and repetitious digging and panning never ceased while there was daylight. The excitement among them was high, but Cupun was uneasy as he had not registered a claim or any land in his name, and he had an annoying sense that they were being watched from far away. It was just after sunset that Cupun worried further about someone outside of their group stumbling upon them so he instructed his daughter that it would behoove her to bury their gold findings under a hidden rock.

Willie Dresen had arrived to St. Michael in 1928 and well enough after the Nome Gold Rush years that he felt he had some making up to do for lost time. To slither his fingers past the larynx reaching further down and yanking out the treasure of thy neighbor's toil was Willie's specialty, and to exploit any opportunity was Willie's desire and ambitious limits.

As a young fisherman along the riverbanks, Willie told his best friend the story of squatting behind shrubbery for several hours not a stone's throw away from Cupun and the three gold prospectors, and how he watched them dynamite and labor, and when he returned behind that shrubbery at first light they were already mining again. He would tell how the noise from the rapids would prevent him from hearing their conversations but he assumed they had amassed a payout, and it was that afternoon that he stayed low and followed them out. Not a day later Willie had broken into Cupun's cabin and began rummaging for the gold findings. He looked in jars and throughout all of Cupun's belongings but it was not to be found. In desperation he plotted to hide under the bed and wait for someone to return home and perhaps give clue to the stash of gold, and then he'd ambush. Willie carried a pocketknife and agreed with himself that if there was a hidden safe that he would wait for the moment it opened and charge with knife stabbing. He took a peek underneath the bed and there stowed the Oosik, a strange object to Willie. He paused to contemplate his serendipitous discovery and pondered his thoughts to this endeavor; would he have to hide it or move away with it? Could this enrich his opportunities? He convinced himself that he would not tell his girlfriend how he found it and he hoped that he could keep it a secret long enough. His moment of frozen thrill thrust forward as he ran away from the cabin with the Oosik.

For six years later, Willie had told the story of how he acquired the Oosik many times to his ever changing crew aboard his commercial fishing boat, where he captained and docked out of Cold Bay, Alaska. His story was that of one lucky man hearing dynamite and upon closer examination seeing the Oosik stuck between rocks of a riverbed. It's told that while out at sea, Willie would brandish the Oosik as a weapon to smack his catch in the head and to motivate his crew he would yell at them, "Catch me something big enough and I'll bring down the Oosik."

Sanford Tinius had given his least effort while laboring at the salmon cannery and during his short three-week tenure there, his boss would not once graduate him to freedom outside working on the loading dock. Sanford was to remain on the assembly line, both indoors and supervised. Those three weeks of enmity between his attitude and his employer were for him about to snap, until he was hired-on to the boat by Willie Dresen for the adventure of being out on the open sea and for better pay.

Sanford, the vagabond grunt, was seasick from the afternoon of the first day until the boat returned to harbor with its full load one week later. Sanford had remained on his backside in bed rolling with the waves and not eating and certainly not working, and worse, he knew that there would be no money placed into his hand when it was time for payout.

It was shortly after dinner on June 18, 1934, a Monday, when Willie returned to his boat and saw that the Oosik was missing from its usual spot. The report he filed with the harbor police pinned the suspect to be Sanford. Willie went on to explain, "I allowed him up on the bridge just one time when he came up to give notice that he would have to depart once we got back to dock."

Sanford had made an excuse for himself that Willie did not deserve the Oosik nor had he treated it with its due respect. With Willie onshore negotiating his catch with the buyer, and the crew removing the fish from the ice box, Sanford snuck himself up to the bridge. When his fingers felt the bone's robust grandeur for the first time he knew this would alleviate the pain of a busted trip to Alaska. He had no time for examination and quickly finessed it down inside his trousers and overcoat until it hit a knee and reached up to his shoulder. He walked off the boat and had the nerve to thank Willie for the opportunity.

The Oosik most definitely bounced around the seat of Sanford's Sedan as it was driven along treacherous roads at speeds barely suitable for such a wagon, and he was already scheming a story as to why he became owner of the Oosik, and decided to tell his family, once he got back home, that because the catches were so minuscule the captain had given him the Oosik as compensation for such low pay. Later, during this hustle to cross the border out of Alaska, he settled on a new lie in which he had rescued it from inside a burning tavern, a fire that sadly the bar owner perished in. Sanford was set on racing himself back home to David City, Nebraska to work on his parents' farm as his next viable option, and damn, it was only two months earlier when he had sworn to never work in a corn field again.

The Oosik lived inside a tiny two-bedroom house at 36 Austin Rd., in Prince George, Canada for one week that summer. A dental office now sits on the site where that old house was torn down.

The Oosik was well outside of Alaska when Ellie Gibb had flagged him down, and when Sanford agreed to give hitchhiker Ellie a ride home. She was in a hurry to reach her parents' house before her father passed away. He had fallen and suffered a head injury and was in coma. Sanford told her that he would drive his best to get her to Prince George. The distance was two days.

Sanford delivered her home and was shown into the backroom where the father lay unconscious. There was a mother without savings, and the house did not receive any relatives paying their respects.

Sanford had already begun an affair with Ellie based on their mutual loneliness, and she shared her bedroom with him for a week. In the beginning he fretted himself over where to store the Oosik, hidden in the Sedan or inside the house with him. As the week wore on he eventually did share his treasure with Ellie and her mother, but when he drove into town for supplies or a rest at the tavern he definitely carried it along. He was paranoid of thieves breaking into his Sedan so he brought it into his newest haunt, and while enjoying his beer he attempted a four finger twirl of the Oosik, like a majorette twirling a baton, which caught the amusement of another patron who offered a purchase price of one-hundred fifty Canadian cash.

Sanford had waited a week to be alone with the old man in the back room, and his opportunity had finally presented itself. For that whole week Sanford had heard stories about what was important to the old man and what worried him as well, enough stories that Sanford had a general feel for the man. Whatever was about to happen, he didn't want to be admonished by the ladies if his efforts seemed unscrupulous, so with Ellie and her mother away from the house, Sanford mustered up all his assertiveness and stood over the man clapping loudly and yelling, "Fire, Money, Ellie." He was determined to startle the old man and snap him out of his coma. He yelled, "It's your dad!" and with that he saw facial movement.

Sanford placed a damp wash cloth over the man's forehead and left the house without any good-byes. He and the Oosik were on a crusade for Nebraska.

If the rumors he heard were correct, and he assumed so, then absolutely they were about to deviate course. Sanford and the Oosik arrived in South Dakota just in time to start jackhammering the head and face of Thomas Jefferson on Mount Rushmore.

The name Sanford Tinius was first entered into the employee ledger on July 9 of 1934, and he was one of the first laborers to carve out an eye, however, it was quickly apparent that he was no artist, so he was sent to the backside of the monument to jackhammer a long tunnel with a secret room.

Many years later, I was one of the lucky few tourists that were led through that site by Mount Rushmore superintendent, Janet Archbold, as she told the story of that hidden chamber; it included the efforts of Sanford Tinius, and with the Oosik that was always nearby. She described how Sanford was usually alone while he labored and chiseled out that granite for nearly two years digging out that secret room, which was located in the back of Abraham Lincoln's head, and was designed to house America's most important paperwork, for a future society to discover. She shared the jokes passed down from that era that other employees thought the Oosik should remain sealed inside the chamber along with the paperwork. Janet showed me where Sanford and the Oosik lived at that time with two pack mules in a wooden shack atop that mountain, which was long ago torn down.

"He was outdoors and he had minimal supervision. It was two good years for him," she told me. On Sundays he would venture off the mountain to play in the employee baseball tournaments, and the others would joke that he should use the Oosik to bat. It was also suggested to Sanford that he cut a tobacco hole into the Oosik.

"We could smoke through a penis bone inside of Lincoln's head," they laughed.

There was a specific Sunday when Sanford was perplexed on his decision to bring, or not to bring, the Oosik with him off the mountain. That was the Sunday of his baptism. He was considering holding the Oosik during the moment of accepting Christ.

It was that same Sunday when nobody at the baseball games or from inside the church thought anything alarming about the two rifle shots they had heard from atop the monument. An elk hunter, Sheb Grubb, who was carrying a half full bottle of cheap wine, had seen two brown objects near Sanford's wooden shack, and he shot twice. Sheb stood over what were two large moose, and he was in a confused state as he wasn't absolute if they were elk or moose. He couldn't tell the difference. He considered the arduous task of cutting off one head and dragging it to basecamp for someone else to identify the species, but after convincing himself that their snouts were just too long to be elk he chose to abandon both dead animals where they lay.

Around the time while Sanford was receiving the Holy Spirit, his door to the shack was being swung open. Sheb knew the instant he saw the Oosik laid out on the table that it was his for the keeping. He left his wine bottle on top of that table.

They sat around their campfire and they had no idea what the Oosik was. Sheb was showing it off to members of his hunting party, and after thorough examinations they could not determine with certainty if it was ivory or not, or what animal it probably had come from, no ideas. The thirteen notches were a pointless nothing to them, and the two carvings were just a purposeless mystery. If collectively they would have been just a degree dumber, they would have used it as their fire poker stick.

Shed returned home to Sioux Falls, South Dakota and right away made arrangements to meet his favorite girlfriend, Dorothy Sollers. Sheb had, for quite some time, imagined and desired that Dorothy would become more involved with him than she already was; he wanted to win her for himself, but so did others. Dorothy liked working at the brothel, and she didn't mind that Sheb romanced her outside as well, but she was not a one-guy kind of gal.

Dorothy would later say of Sheb, "He liked after sex pillow-talk, whisper his secrets, he couldn't shut up." She was the best source to clear up any rumors floating around about the Oosik and to report on just how obsessed Sheb had become with getting it back. He had recently made a bad trade.

Dorothy would say, "He became crazy shortly after seeing Opal."

Sheb had brought the Oosik into negotiate a sale price with Opal Vandercook, who owned both Opal's Mercantile and the connecting Opal's Grain & Seed. Her little business had started out years before as Opal's Trading Post and since grew along with her savvy business skills into the establishment where most everything needed in Sioux Falls, outside of automotive parts, could be purchased through thrifty Opal.

Opal asked Sheb how he got it. He answered, "A fight."

It was an exceptionally hot summer throughout South Dakota, a record breaking heat wave, and Sheb was impatient to get some cash and get somewhere cooler. He figured to buy beers and take Dorothy to the river just as soon after Opal quit examining the Oosik and made him an offer.

"I can give you $23."

Sheb prepared to eagerly accept but felt obliged to hesitate to give Opal the feeling that she was definitely taking advantage of him.

Opal struck first, "That's the $18.50 you already owe me, plus a new store credit of $4.50."

"At least I can get beer," he realized.

"It's a deal," she demanded.

The Oosik was hung resting on two nails pounded in the wall behind her cash register, and Opal would enjoy when patrons asked her questions about the long boney object.

For the first two months of ownership, Opal remained perplexed about that Oosik, and when folks would ask her for details she would kindly retort with an invitation for them to guess, and that was her ploy to hopefully uncover for herself any new facts.

In was in August of the same summer, after selling beads to an insightful customer from Rosebud Sioux Tribe, that she could finally tell the curious, with some details, that it was an Oosik, and after she had learned that the Oosik was a penis bone, she would tell her customers, "It's my cold-cocker. Shoplift from me and I'll cold-cock you with it."

The McKinley High drama club had created a play entitled, "Twas the Night for a Snake Oil Charmer," and billed it as a Christmas theme with a twist. One of the seniors and actresses in that drama club was a cousin to Opal Vandercook, who had taken loan of the Oosik to be a prop in that play.

On the snowy afternoon of 24 December, the parents had been ushered into the gymnasium and were witness to a bizarre opening act whereas a former Chinese railway worker, who had become a snake oil salesman, was waving the Oosik above his head and yelling to women passing by on the street, "Stop feeling your monthly!" The unsuspecting women were lured to his side, where he confessed, "Powder ground up from this walrus penis bone is the only elixir you women need." He would go onto to describe how he had shaved off this medicine into a fine powder, which sold by the gram. He waved the Oosik again, like a soaring eagle's wing, and assured his female audience that their ailments would from now on be pain free. With the first woman opening her purse, he pointed at the Oosik and bellowed, "These thirteen notches are evidence from university scholars who tested the authenticity and the density of the medicine as proof of its high potency." The purses were opening as he yelled across the street to more women, "You won't feel your monthly!" The conflicted pastor, played by a frail freshman, rushes the stage in an attempt to stop the deleterious scamster and save the soul of this Chinese profiteer, all while we soon discover his wife is dying in hospital after a failed kidney surgery. The pastor lunges to grab hold of the Oosik and a tug a war ensues. This was succeeded by the two badgering back and forth about female physiology and profound statements were used to one-up the other, and with whomever was holding the Oosik was clearly the wiser and more familiar about womanly needs.

Sitting in the audience was Sheb Grubb watching his estranged daughter act the part of an unfortunate sucker with abdominal cramps, and each time the Oosik was shown as the keystone prop he became increasingly mindful and agitated that he was known as the infamous desperate fool that had bartered it away.

Between Act 2 and Act 3 with the curtain down, a scattering of upset parents were already headed home and some would later refuse to acknowledge the blasphemous satire because they expected, and did not want to accept, a worn-down hypocritical pastor running off with a pinch of that magical dust. The Oosik would be returned atop those two nails at Opal's store.

On New Year's Eve, a widowed mother alone in Eau Claire, Wisconsin worried for her two children who were driving west through the night, and her angst would heighten for two more weeks until she received her first telephone call as to their whereabouts and as to their wellbeing, That phone call shared an appareny that they were getting along quite well together, and that their mutual obsession with moving somewhere in the Rocky Mountains and finding jobs was transpiring as well as the two siblings had hoped. Mother had given them their deceased father's Studebaker for the drive west, and she offered for them to sell it if they ran out of money.

John and June Corsault were chasing the setting sun west with illusions of mysterious mountain thickets dense with deer, and wild goats with curved horns, all in their imaginations from their father's bedtime stories. Probably John was driving as he was the eager ninth grade dropout with his first driver's license and the more enthusiastic of the two, although June was two years his elder and she was the steadier of the siblings. By all accounts, it was said that both were beautiful to look at. They drove into the darkness with wool blankets wrapped around their legs against the winter chill, and maybe they were laughing, and maybe they were listening to the car radio. They had hatched this rendezvous with the Rockies over one year earlier and it was now Day 1 of its fruition with dreams of any type of job they could grab, work on a cattle farm or as a cook; any job sounded wonderful. Unfortunately however, it was winter and they knew their chances of quick employment would be difficult to secure.

Sheb had the streets of downtown almost to himself that same evening, and it would have been deathly quiet except for the swing band he could hear playing from inside the ballroom at Cataract Hotel just a couple blocks away from where he stood hiding in the dark. He probably felt himself secretly alone in the city, a feeling he needed because he was stalking Opal. He waited for her to close and lock up the stores. It had been exactly one week ago when that play had ended and he needed to make things right for himself. He hid in the shadows and watched her thick set of brass keys drop into her pockets as she started her way home. He would give himself five minutes to assess the situation while building up the courage to kick in her door.

Sheb could not have known during those moments that a small group of criminals three miles east of town had dumped a freshly dead body alongside of four to five thousand pounds of dynamite, and over one thousand kegs of blasting powder and had just ignited a fuse long enough to burn while they ran away, in what would later be called the Powder House explosion. The crater from that blast would measure fifty-feet wide and twenty-five feet deep, and it was felt over one-hundred miles away and registered on seismographs in California. However, more relevant to a shocked and determined Sheb was the fact that every storefront window near him had miraculously shattered from that explosion, leaving his prize only a few unhindered steps within reach.

John and June were driving the flat plains a few miles east of Sioux Falls when they first saw the fiery ball in the sky and felt the loud concussion against their car. They stopped roadside and stepped outside to reign in their fears, "Were we shot at, and is that where we're going tonight?" must have been their initial concerns.

Sheb was seen running out of Opal's with the Oosik in his hand and attempting a getaway over glass and brick by Dannen, the only cop left not yet in route to the explosion. Sheb was apprehended and placed in the back seat of the patrol car; his creative thoughts were destroyed which cleared way for a new creation. Sheb was locked into a cell and the Oosik quickly logged in as evidence before Dannen left to join the investigation at the explosion.

Inside room 301 at the Cataract Hotel were June and John. June was occupied with affixing a blanket to cover the broken window and John sat on his bed trying to meditate away his fears of a most brazen act from just moments earlier when he entered the abandoned police station to inquire about the blast and saw the Oosik sitting atop a desk. He had sensed he was alone and an all too familiar impulse rushed through him to immediately take whatever he saw and to do it quickly. He had a history of stealing, which started with bubblegum as a kid as a moment of exhilarated compulsive thrills. John saw the Oosik for a dollar value and a means to get something for it. He heard a whimpering from the back cell, it was Sheb pleading, "Let me out of here." John made eye contact and exited with the Oosik.

John pushed the Oosik deep into a sidewalk snowbank alongside of the police station, a snowbank only ten feet from the desktop it was sitting on only thirty-seconds prior. The Oosik would have to hide overnight in the snow which would give him enough time to strategize.

He had swiped something that belonged to someone else and he regretted it and feared any of the consequences, if he had been seen; otherwise maybe it was a good move, he concluded. He found a calming frame of mind in preparation that if someone knocked at their door during the night he could appear tranquil and innocent.

In the morning, and only after he was sure that they were leaving town, did he return to the Oosik. He met up with his June waiting at their car and gleefully told her, "Look what I just found." By lunchtime the Oosik had passed over Lewis & Clark's trail and was heading west towards the Rocky Mountains.

Dorothy would later testify that she waited at home with the lights off and in fear all night for Sheb to return with the Oosik.

This clipping was retrieved from the archives of The Daily newspaper:

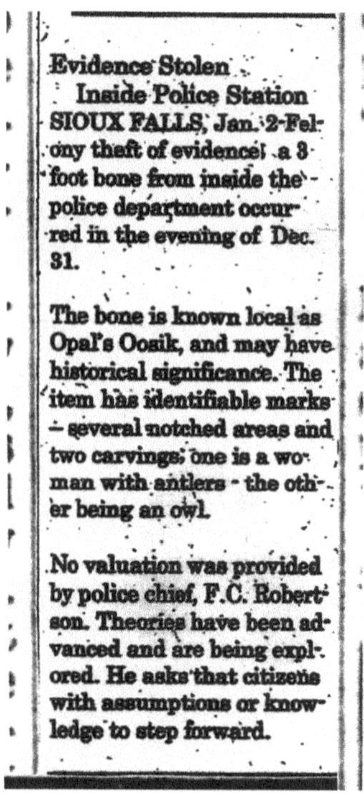

Evidence Stolen
Inside Police Station
SIOUX FALLS, Jan. 2-Felony theft of evidence; a 3-foot bone from inside the police department occurred in the evening of Dec. 31.

The bone is known local as Opal's Oosik, and may have historical significance. The item has identifiable marks - several notched areas and two carvings; one is a woman with antlers - the other being an owl.

No valuation was provided by police chief, F.C. Robertson. Theories have been advanced and are being explored. He asks that citizens with assumptions or knowledge to step forward.

The Oosik was accepted to John and June as their good luck charm and it tagged along with them through several one-day stops in small Colorado towns, which was just enough time for them to get a sense of belonging. They ended their westward journey in the picturesque and mountainous town of

Buena Vista where the Oosik resided on the second level of their two-bedroom flat with a pot-belly heat stove.

June took a clerical job at the courthouse, and shortly before summer, John started working at The Diamond Hitch, which was a boy's camp with an outdoor swimming pool.

The Oosik would see June go through a courtship, which led to marriage and her moving out of the flat. The Oosik would watch John become a river rafting guide and a horse trail guide. During their second year in Buena Vista, John became a welder and artist, and he put the two crafts together when a left over object was welded onto another weird object, and if it was strange enough it might sell.

John enjoyed volunteering his Wednesday nights calling Bingo for the old ladies, and he always brought the Oosik with him to stir up the basket of Bingo balls before each game. For him it was about making women laugh.

John slid a rubber end-cap onto the bottom of the Oosik and used it as a cane while he faked an injury and limped through town and used it as a subject matter to meet and flirt with new prospective women. And the many women he did meet! The Oosik had a ringside seat during all the bouts with the various beauties John brought back to their flat. John would eventually expand his game by telling additional prospective women that each of the Oosik's thirteen notches, which he told them were carved by him, represented a tribute of the thirteen girls that he had slept with during their first date under the stars at his favorite and hidden spot along the river. He would describe the honorary membership in joining his Oosik Club in such a manner that overwhelmed their inquisitiveness and tempted their considerations into earning a notch of their own. John personified a young man writing his own rules.

For three and one-half years the Oosik and John lived that status-quo, the philanderer and the cane, and his friends nicknamed him Johnny 14, and then the U.S. instituted an Act that he would have to register for the draft, thus ending the lifestyle he had built for himself. John didn't want to leave the mountains, he didn't want to conform, and he certainly was too scared to be anywhere near a frontline of a war; in fact the Oosik had never seen him in a fight. John was a pacifist by nature and a lover of nature, and so he prepared his plan to not enlist. He was acquainted with Bret McNabb, who ran the local draft board, and John found him in a casual setting one afternoon and showed him the Oosik, and where he made Bret this offer, "If my name is not entered into the draft for one year or if my name is rejected, then in one year's time I will give this to you." John hoped that after a full year of army drafting, they would have enough recruits that they would stop before he was needed. Bret was bestowed with great powers as it pertained to the draft, and he was enjoying the visuals on the Oosik as they shook hands with a gentlemen's agreement and noted that the day was 14 September.

By May, the Oosik was freed from its rubber end-cap and John himself was released from his dependence on the cane during a rebirthing of the Oosik into a sacred object. It would be that same tranquil afternoon during a walk through City Park that the circle of John-the-welder and the Oosik collided with a more selective circle that through most circumstances would have never let them into their bubble. The Sharnowske family had the big-house on top of the hill that allowed them to look down on everyone else, and two years prior to this collision in City Park, they had donated the funds to build and furnish Buena Vista's first museum, and their oldest daughter, Sara Sharnowske, was the museum's first curator.

It was four against one, as the two circles of life neared each other. It was Sara with her two younger brothers strolling through City Park with their father on the first warm day of the year, and it was John, and it was their souls who were finally ready to meet. Sara and John met each other in the eyes and their mutual past had returned before them. What started as a de' ja vu turned into a quiet peace that buried in their history they had shared a past life together and even lived together. Into a simple jump into the future they would soon be finishing each other's sentences, but for the moment it was the rarest of cosmic encounters where an overdose of dopamine and the release of endorphins flooded their brains and opiate receptors shut down their final sense of balance causing them both to faint and collapse to the grass. Maybe the two brothers were quick to fight with this intruder that somehow knocked their sister to the ground, but the father innately manifested this weakness as the origin of love and instructed his two sons to aid their sister while he helped John back to his feet.

There was one week during that summer, with Sara sick in her bed, that she handed John the keys to the museum and instructed him to collect the 20 cent admission and for him to watch over the guests. John would be surrounded by collectables and artifacts that throughout his being he would salivate at the chance to relocate such items to his personal address.

On John's first morning at the museum he simply watched folks as they read each placard and he was utterly bored, then once school was let out he received a surprise visit from the Sharnowske's ten year old daughter, Bodil, who ritualized doing her homework at the museum and talking with Sara, but now it was John for her to befriend.

Bodil had dropped her school bag onto the counter next to John and made it clear to him that she would be a permanent staple each afternoon until she chose to go home. Bodil had unloaded a couple of book in preparation to study.

John saw something unfitting inside her bag," What's that book?"

A smirk, "my teacher's grade book."

"Why do you have it?"

A shrug of the shoulders.

Before that afternoon ended, John had penciled-in an improved grade for Bodil and a relationship was cemented.

On the second afternoon in the museum, Bodil presented two stolen items; another kid's magic kit and the spelling homework from her entire class, both of which she had found time to swipe during a play break. That was the same afternoon that John discovered a means to rid his boredom and humor himself by displaying the Oosik in the museum and creating its own placard, *Milky Way Toothpick — Unearthed with Meteor Rocks - $10,000*. The guests would gasp in amazement and call their families to hurry over, and for John and Bodil to watch those stunned faces stare into their trick with awe and bewilderment made for the most exciting moments during a long afternoon.

On the following days at the museum it was Bodil's responsibility to pull something from her history book to give title to the Oosik. One day it was a White Forest Venomous Sea Slug from the depths of the Arctic, another day it was part of a dinosaur dug up at the end of a rainbow, and each day that week a new item had been confiscated and stolen by Bodil and brought in for show and tell: someone else's art homework and another kid's science project, and John had considered penning a letter to the school exposing the whole story, but he didn't, and he lacked the moxie and skillset to tell her parents, so he didn't. "What if something went missing from the museum?" he thought, "Yes, they would blame me."

In July of 1941, John believed that Sara already knew whatever he was thinking before a word could leave his lips, so out of guilt he confessed to how the Oosik had first come into his possession, and it was her suggestion that they move beyond the Oosik chapter in their lives, and together they sat inside the draft board and presented the Oosik to Bret McNabb, which was two months earlier than he was expecting to take ownership.

Navajo Indian Reservation – Outside of Santa Fe, New Mexico

Bret arrived without invitation on the third afternoon of a four day Blessingway of song and prayer for rain, and he sat in the wilderness with the Navajo elders who were telling their story of Four Worlds to the children with the consequences if they didn't treat earth and others with respect. The children all huddled together along a creek and heard this most important teaching that included many animals and monsters and would normally take an entire afternoon to complete.

They were told of the First World as a dark and unhappy place, inhabited by bugs, and where the creation of man and woman were hatched from eggs and not yet in human form, and that they would fail many times to find each other, until they did, and to escape this misery their spirits flew out of a hole in the east and landed in the Second World, which was blue and inhabited by dangerous people, and man and woman were unhappy and hungry there, so with the help of a tall growing plant they were lifted into the Third World, which had water and mountains and harmony, but only for a short while, with other people, until disease came and man fought with woman over chores and sex, so they separated themselves to different islands, and could only please themselves with inanimate objects, so they were lonely and decided to once again live together, but their fighting continued so a storm flooded that world, but just in time a tall plant lifted them up towards the Fourth World ahead of the rising water, but there was great fear because they had to wait for the wind to dry their new world before they could walk on it, and just in time it was ready, and they rose to see the sun, the moon and the stars for the first time, and they became human beings, and they learned that fire would keep them warm.

The story was over, and with the children now understanding that they needed to cherish this world or the consequences were its destruction, Bret passed the Oosik to an elder sitting on a rock at his side. The Oosik was admired by him for its mysteries and it was passed around the circle of elders who rubbed on it and felt the two carvings against their thumbs and the elders broke away from English and spoke Navajo of the Oosik with enthusiasm and rapture as if telling a secret folk tale that they needed to contain in their possession away from Bret. The last to feel the Oosik was James Oliver Jr., a twenty year old phenomenon that Bret had come specifically to recruit as a Code Talker for the Marine Corp.

Bret had been transferred from Colorado to Fort Wingate, New Mexico to utilize his skills in recruiting young Navajo men with their complex language to create a code that the Japanese military could not break or translate, which would give the U.S. military the needed ability and advantage to communicate its actions with surprise.

There were twenty-eight other Navajo men that had recently enlisted, but it was James Oliver Jr. that Bret wanted the most, as he epitomized what the program needed; high aptitude, memory like an elephant, proven teamwork and decision making skills, top of his class in calculus, outperformed everyone else during a survival training course, and on hunts with the elders he had the ability to flank the prey, deer and elk, and complete several kills without the herd having any awareness of his presence, and Bret knew he wanted to attend college, so for Bret is was like recruiting the state's fastest runner for the track team, and this incentive of substantial reward was offered to James Oliver Jr.: "The Oosik is yours in exchange for you helping me as a Code Talker."

In August of 1942, the Oosik was stored inside the log hogan of James' mother while Corporal James Oliver Jr. saw the ocean waves for his time while on deployment to the South Pacific theater of battle as radio man translating tactical messages into secret code that he had created, which included his special words, such as turtle of tank, iron fish for submarine and Oosik (penis) for sniper, which were used to coordinate battles, big and small: at Guadalcanal, it was used in the Philippines, and finally on Iwo Jima.

During the three years that James was away humping a radio on his back, the Navajo medicine man would occasionally retrieve and use the Oosik for ceremonial burials, which was waved over the dead body as a means to satisfy their spirit and comfort the body during its journey to the afterlife, but most importantly to keep their ghost from returning to this world, the Fourth World, and haunting the living with its evil spirits.

Before the arrival of the Oosik, the Navajo had immense fear of a deceased soul, even fearing the almost dead so much that words were not spoken of the dead, but post Oosik the burial rituals were modified because of the thirteen notches. There were only symbolic meanings for the numbers one through twelve, but the thirteen notches were woven into folklore as the protector of the living from the dead. The Oosik was the medicine man's best tool, so much so that it became the only item that was allowed to return with the living after a ceremony, and all other items such as the spirit wheel of the dead and the hatchet were burnt so any lingering bad spirits could not follow them home.

James did return home after the surrender, where he studied at a community college, married and raised one son, while working his way up to senior officer at Citizen Bank in Bloomfield, New Mexico.

For a chasm of time spanning twenty years after his return home the Oosik was used so often by several medicine men that James hung it in a slip knot that dangled from the awning near the front door of his own log hogan so that it could easily be taken on loan.

He was 29 year old Seoras Surratt, and this particular morning he was chewing several peyote buttons, he swallowed the bitterness, and while resting on his blanket lying on the desert basin he gazed into the beauty of Fajada Butte; which would one day become a World Heritage Site and National Park, but for now he waited for the oncoming vomit, which came twice, and then the euphoria. The colors of nature became brighter and a waterfall fed a new river of pea green soup flowing within reach should he kneel down for an afternoon craving of nutrients, and he could see the wind as it positioned itself near one ear and built up strength in a wheat-gold color that deafened as it massaged through his inner-head and passed out the other ear.

There was added clarity to his thoughts as he realized that he did have the untapped-power to make himself invisible to other humans. Seoras climbed a couple of colossal and steep rocks that were actually no higher than four feet, and for a moment he pondered why he was still trapped in selecting what to do for his own future, which was an irritating thought, so he replaced it with thoughts of his last wife, who was raised by Romanian gypsies and because she was seeking citizenship she lassoed herself a man, him, and four years earlier Seoras married that sweetheart, so he had always thought, but the ceremony was a fraud, the certificate was a fraud and the minister was a nobody but a paid transient, because it was all a ruse by her and a friend because she didn't really desire to marry him, except she imagined that he had shown potential to provide an upscale lifestyle, but he couldn't keep a job, so after three years she was gone along with many of his possessions, and he still wasn't clear on her motives, which was now a dark and maddening thought.

He pushed those thoughts aside and watched a brown hawk circle him overhead before swooping down for a conversation.

"You will be a great leader, a leader of many, in politics or if you are too impatient then a cult leader," said the brown hawk.

Seoras saw himself as cult leader of likeminded misogynistic peyote-cravers that would band together in rebuke of the ridiculous idea of matrimony with only a single woman for life.

"What do you hope for the most?" asked the brown hawk.

"I wish to be invisible."

"You are invisible."

"I want to perform various acts of fun that can only be done if I'm invisible. I want to walk freely amongst large stacks of cash. I will remove money from banks."

Seoras rested his head later that night in a jail cell, and the story he will thereafter tell will begin while he's driving thirty minutes north on highway 550 at the crescendo of his peyote adventure.

On that same midday that Seoras was driving north and ascending on Bloomfield, so was Mr. Walde Beadles, a motorcycle mechanic from Arizona, who scoured through classifieds and obituaries for unusual deals. He had left his house, along with his wife, in the early hours to buy a bright red 1964 convertible C2 Corvette with black interior for only $500, which was valued at over $20,000, but the young man who owned it had recently died in Vietnam and his mother, the seller, was oblivious to its market value. If the car was still there when they arrived, and Walde hoped to be the first to arrive, then Walde intended to hand her the cash and leave as soon as the paperwork was signed.

Seoras walked into an already busy bank and went unnoticed through the lobby, past the teller line and past the restroom, where he paused and envisioned what this was going to look like to the employees; there will be large stack of cash that he would be carrying, but to them it would be suspended in the air and floating so mysteriously towards the entrance. While he waited for the gate to the vault to be opened he wandered to the back of house where the employees ate their meals, and there he saw the Oosik on the eating table.

The eighteen year old son of James, who was working for his father as a teller, had brought in the Oosik as a show-and-tell to the other employees, and left it in the lounge after lunch.

Seoras interpreted the Oosik being left unattended as a message that it would be needed for his upcoming cult seminars and grabbed it for his taking. He was just minutes from leaving the bank when he walked behind the teller line and pulled open a cash drawer; it was empty and before he could grab ahold of another drawer two lady employees were both yelling at him in a feverish pitch, so he left the bank without any cash.

Walde was driving through Bloomfield in his new Corvette when through fortuitous circumstances he sees Seoras also driving out of town and being chased by one police car with siren blaring. Feeling lucky and always the opportunist, Walde followed the action in close pursuit. Seoras was almost out of town and nearing a bridge over a dried river wash when paranoia overwhelmed his senses, and needing to lose the evidence, he flings the Oosik out his passenger window and figures to circle back and recover it on a different day. The Oosik fell twenty feet below that bridge and ricocheted off shrubs before landing next to sand sage. To Walde, it looked like a gun had been thrown out the window, and he let the pursuing police car get out of his sight before pulling off the roadway.

The Oosik was found and placed into the trunk of the mint condition Corvette and quickly driven away. Walde took it back to his home to Kino Springs, Arizona, near the border with Mexico, and wrapped it inside a of a large burlap bag once used to hold potatoes, and tucked it away inside his backyard shed where it would rest for nearly forty-three years.

II

The death of a sailor from a shipyard explosion triggered the events of a group that thrust themselves into a collision with history, which culminated in the revival of that resting relic.

I decided this story, of that group about to form, needed to start at the aftermath of a fiery death to a young man while serving in the Coast Guard, then to his father, Peter Beneventi, making an impulsive decision that would lead to the second renaissance of the Oosik.

Peter was completing the sale of his favorite toy, a four-seat Cessna Skyhawk airplane for two reasons; first he needed some extra cash to pay off the taxes and late fees to his deceased son's house, and secondly because his head-dizzying vertigo was intensifying with each turbulent bounce to the point that the hobby had become quite unpleasant. Peter had lost not only his favorite pastime and his only child, but he was now stricken with panic that his life would become meaningless inertia until he quickly discovered a new hobby that would assuage those painful losses.

During his short drive from the tarmac to his home in Walnut Creek, California, Peter had all but settled on a smidgen of the profits to be spent exploring earth, a trip around the world.

He had no one inherently left to coordinate with, how simple, and his excitement to chart a new course led him to cast out an invite, so onto his Facebook page and to convey his life changing idea with alacrity that would captivate the curious, "To any and all my FB friends with a passport," he wrote, "I am creating an adventure to begin next June around the world.

Let's start in Myanmar and travel west for several weeks, perhaps exploring many exotic countries. Commitments due in January for Visas and deposits. Please email me direct if you want to be part of the planning."

Peter was a spare-bedroom entrepreneur in the early conception of the dot com era and hadn't clocked-in at an office for years since his launch of "Firstdate," a platform to share your profound experiences concerning a past lover, which in return allowed the next unsuspecting lover a historical examination prior to their upcoming candlelit rendezvous; posts were positive and negative, predominantly the later. The second shingle Peter hung from his house was another online creation, "Trackers," whereas he would randomly select one adult from the lower forty-eight states, show up at their house and offer them the opportunity to slap on his GPS ankle bracelet and within thirty minutes "go on the run for one week like a fugitive," while his three hired professional trackers and anyone else in the United States was looking for the criminal. A successful week on the run was a million dollar prize, and anyone that found the criminal before the weeks' end would become the million dollar winner themselves, but lack of corporate sponsorship and liability concerns have kept Trackers sidelined. Peter's first bullseye winner was using his myriad of stock news footage to superimpose his client's image onto scenes showing them performing heroic acts, such as pulling a dolphin across the beach into the waves, helping a fellow skydiver untangle their parachute just moments before certain death, or whatever his client had ever fantasized was now possible. Often a fee of $10,000 was paid to Vain Videos by a client receiving a compilation of stories meant to entertain guests or salvage a prosaic dinner date.

Peter was determined not to allow the hassles of life to sideline his now spontaneous need to see more of the world, and that meant to him, if he needed to be a solo traveler because his post went unanswered, then that was fine with him.

Dr. Joan Bendimez worked independently from her home in Seattle as a consultant to Big Pharma on how they can get their drug through trial and eventually approved by the FDA. She was also part of a successfully secret group that for the past thirty years profited each member well over the amount needed to put the kids through college, but just last week that secret group voted to dismantle and payout the dividends. Joan had long ago been part of a mammoth 1980 graduation class at Kentridge High School, about a half hour south of Seattle, and by the time many of them were graduating from college they coalesced as an investment group with exclusivity to their class. The clandestine investors spoke regularly and met annually to vote on new investments and when to trade; there had been emergency conference calls to argue and persuade the group's portfolio, and there had been some lean years but the cleverness of the collective mass had raised their value to remarkable gains. Joan had always felt a proud sense of accomplishment that the group had appeared to keep their original charter promise to never share a whisper about their secret group to any relative or even a spouse. Equaling her pride with the group's endeavors was the fact that they had protected their own and sailed through twenty-nine years together at not once been named in a divorce settlement or attached with defendant in a lawsuit. Their meetings had been formal and dour by nature but at the moment of adjournment they broke into a festive assembly of friends that genuinely cared for one another after years of sublime trust. They were now "getting old" and couldn't pass along the torch, so it was unanimous to cease the experiment. One chapter of Joan's life was now closed.

After Joan read Peter's email about traveling the world, she knew she would be going. She wanted to open a new chapter. Her marriage to her college sweetheart gave her great satisfaction, and he would understand her passion for the unknown, and she felt comforted that Peter would melt together a cohesive group of explorers that she needed to be a part of. Peter had also been in a member of that secret investment group, so they both graduated from Kentridge class of 1980, and she felt safe with Peter. Throughout High School she was good at gymnastics and she played various horn instruments in the Jazz Ensemble. Though she was not close friends with Peter back in the school days, she remembered him in choir before he was kicked-out of choir for not being serious.

When Leslie Bishop described her paradigm at the moment of accepting Peter's idea of travel, it was her need to force some shifts, for she was tiring of the frequent arguing with her daughter struggling to find her identity and inner calm; to be vegan, to be transgender, what is spiritual growth and is chakra real? These things were stuck without resolution and Leslie needed an escape. Leslie had been volunteering as a means to find sanctuary away from the family, and her husband undoubtedly was too busy for such a once in a lifetime adventure. These complaints were normal family irritants, but the real shift she needed that was draining her energies was a contract lying on her table that she wasn't eager to sign as a prelude to selling her business. In Leslie's early years of marriage she sold jars of her raw bee honey at farmer's markets and street fairs throughout Portland, and her talents grew in later years to extracting cannabis oils for her own edible bars. The demand quickly became overwhelming. Now her cannabis farm was for sale and she wanted more than offered and figured that a few weeks disappearing on a trip around the world would send a loud message that she was not all that interested in their offering price. Leslie had attended the same elementary school and middle school that many of her classmates from Kentridge High class of 1980 had also attended during their childhood, and she was remembered for playing piano in school competitions, earned her place in honors roll, and was admired by the boys in middle school for being perhaps the first to reach puberty with those breasts. The boys had swarmed around her beauty.

Catherine Anastasi was as outspoken and influential about the travel itinerary as she had so often been during those secret investment group meetings when she was articulate and demanding and always prepared. Catherine was keen for detail and strove for a beautiful result, just like an aesthetician should. She had a voracious appetite for research and she controlled the arduous planning of hotels and reserving the many excursions.

With her thumb on the schedule, Catherine was able to coincide their trip with her husband's plan to construct an addition to the house for her mother-in-law, something she certainly didn't desire or intend to project manage. She thought of herself as a faithful Catholic wife that knew where to draw a line in the sand, and in this case, she wanted her husband alone in the sandbox with the frustrating permit delays and unforeseen change orders.

Catherine had given to others so many facials, so many chemical peels, and countless massages over the years that she was due some well-deserved time away from everything familiar with Seattle.

When fanning through the Kentridge High School album, Catherine's picture would cover sections of the varsity gymnastics, her solo performance in the opera, and her standing in the same row as Peter Beneventi while in German Club together.

The personal diary entry of Nancy May on January 3, 2017, "Everything dreamed and hoped for with has Paul fizzled. I will be going on that trip after all, and I applied for my first passport, exciting…"

Monthly statements from the secret investors were never been mailed out; should they fall into prying hands, such as a spouse, it would have ended the secrecy, so Nancy was elated and surprised when her final payout arrived in her mailbox from a group that she hadn't participated with in many years.

During a long ago recession, Nancy had filed for divorce and soon after had lost her job with Boeing, as a parts inspector, and consequently petitioned the secret group to withdrawal her initial investment of $2,200. The group understood her desperate time, although short-sightedness, and in lieu of refunding her investment, they instead decided to pass the hat and collect enough charity to cover her expenses. Nancy was embarrassed and ostracized herself from her classmates dating all the way back to 1992, including boycotts of the many class reunions.

Nancy's raw talents just took an extra while to say hello; twice divorced and four times engaged, she reeducated herself and settled into a third-grade teaching roll in West Seattle. She was now ready to reconnect with those whom she had, "walked those hallways with so long ago," and she was anxious to destroy whatever image they could remember of her.

At the urging of her father back in tenth grade she tried out for the gymnastics team, which was absurdly too introverted for her need to make noise; then her inner engine was finally satisfied when she became a natural percussionist in the symphonic band, which cured her rebel untamed disorders, but not completely, for it was rumored that the circumstances of one particular afternoon in eleventh grade developed in the parking lot for Nancy with joints and loud rock, before making her way, although late, to English class, where she was relentlessly challenged to articulate a prolific feeling on the subject matter; disco music. Nancy, never one for filters, found her poetic response, "it is the hemorrhoid pus in the anus of my adolescent annals," a response which was too offensive for Mrs. Osterhouse, and within the hour Nancy became legendary with being the first female of Kentridge to receive a hack on the ass.

Nancy was the last of the five to sign up for the tour, and concluded her daily journal entry with, "… I am reinvented and confident to step out and show the old classmates my new offerings."

Yangon, Myanmar

A group of five unguarded personalities met in the lobby of Pullman Centrepoint Hotel before breakfast with admiration and surety that their own lives were on the cusp of a nebulous bond of thrills in this oddest of countries, which none of them could have easily found on a map just a few months earlier.

Leslie was the first to comment that everyone looked ageless and was properly dressed for a sultry day in flip-flops and shorts, and Peter boasted that his undergarment white Hanes T shirt were to be the only shirts he'd be wearing, and what he meant was that for the duration of their journey he had one of them for each day and tossed it into the waste basket at the end of each evening. He enjoyed that there would never be a dirty shirt in his travel bag so he had less to carry as the trip progressed.

Their private tour guide and bus shuttled them off precisely at 9am, just as Catherine had scheduled, to the most important Buddhist monument in all of Myanmar, the Shwedagon Pagoda, adorning the skyline with coverings in gold and large diamonds. They had booked the early tour to miss the crowds, but it was already too late, and for two hours inside the Pagoda they inched forward closer to the reliquary containing eight strands of hair from a previous Buddha; a relic to the masses already knelt at the steps of the tiny shrine of such life altering significance that tears and prayers of healing broke all silence and virtue. The group of five would spend much of the morning analyzing and debating how religious relics were spread throughout the world and why they still captivate the devoted and the simple tourist even today.

They wandered through markets buying handicraft and jewelry, specifically necklaces for everyone, and eating spicy street food and pushing back against the oncoming jetlag, until Joan made a decision that would serendipitously alter their purpose beyond Catherine's control. It happened while Nancy and Leslie were the first duet at Karaoke, which was breathtakingly natural and vibrant, and after three consecutive songs it couldn't be hidden that some primal need for expression was jarred loose. Catherine and Joan followed with a duet that transfixed even the bartender long enough to soak up all the beauty. Was an ovation necessary, but it happened to a humbled two that were attached to a momentary time of crystalized bliss. They stood holding hands together and laying out their best as if it were up to them to save music on trial for life. Peter played and entertained that crowd while on a nostalgic rendezvous to once again be that guy singing in his high school garage band, and tonight, he walked that stage like a blood thirsty lion and swung his hips so the girls would laugh. He had selected a song knowing it had dramatic pitch changes and he was hitting all the notes because he wanted to say, "Hey girls, count me in."

Old Bagan, Myanmar

There hangs a framed photo in the lobby of the night-club, Erawati, the first photo taken there, in the ancient village Old Bagan, in a county just recently opened to foreign tourists, that's of such significance to the locals that the events prior to that picture being snapped deserve to be told.

The five had moved north by plane where they rented mopeds from their new hotel, Aye Yar, and set out to explore the land of over 10,000 temples. Their most important investigation was to be inside the stupa that was exhibiting the enamel of Buddha's tooth. It was barely a fragment of visibility but demanded a minimum of ten minutes of awe and discussion.

Their dust-laden faces had made it to their sixth temple just in time for the sunset. They climbed to the top of Ananda Temple where they popped open a bottle of champagne.

During the toast it was Nancy's suggestion, "if we want the spirit of Buddha with us permanently then we need to drink his ashes with our champagne."

Peter whipped out his travel map from his pocket and scribbled the lyric:

I want Buddha ash stirred in champagne
Who would dare complain?
The eternal healing power
I don't care if it tastes sour

Peter wrote the hook:

What price per gram?

The five debated and agreed on a fair black-market value for a gram of Buddha ash and left for dinner at Erawati's; which was celebrating their grand opening that exact evening with a local cover band that was advertised to be playing rock & roll songs from America.

The sound system and equipment were set on stage, but the band's drummer and their lead singer were missing. There was confusion and angst with the other members of the band who were still trying to connect to their band mates via cell phone. It was a suggestion from Nancy to an amenable and desperate lead guitarist that the band start playing with her at drums, and Peter as lead singer, which saved a group named Night of Ruckus from a night of disaster. Peter sang their songs while wondering what his three other travel-mates watching from the audience thought of him, and he struggled for answers as to why at this intense moment he was being so reflective, and well into the third song his thoughts went to retrospective glorious moments when he once sang in a high school garage band. It was agreed, back then, with all the neighbors in a two block radius that they would tolerate his band's loud noise between 4pm and 5:30 in exchange for an occasional street side concert, and with the front row seats always reserved for five old witches, but known to everyone else outside of the band as the Garden Club, which was made up of five senior women who were the anointed judges with the power to rate his songs with a thumbs up or a thumbs down. Those five old witches had a noose around Peter as it was their self-described role to monitor the cleanliness of the neighborhood, and to them rock & roll was a dead shrub, a pot hole in the pavement, and a mound of trash, but that was the agreement Peter had to live with; play well and humor the old bitties. For Nancy back on drums, this was an emotional celebration of reuniting with classmates that have looked down on her as far back as 5th grade, but now she had busted out of her cocoon and tonight her drum rhythms and the closeness of the harmonies were in sweet sync with Peter's vocals. Nancy would catch Peter looking back at her, and she would nod, "Ya, we're this good. Keep going." Peter and Nancy carried Night of Ruckus through a complete a five song set, which ended just after the club owner snapped that picture of them which is now hanging inside the lobby.

Catherine borrowed an acoustic guitar from the band and went straight to her room. Joan called her husband to share her envy for those who had made it onstage.

Catherine wrote a simple lyric about needing the love of friends, and without it, all meaning would come to an end, then she structured it around a simple baseline with a slow tempo. She placed a small wooden chair at the corner of the room and leaned it back against the wall, then positioned her cellphone to capture her moment.

She lit a candle and its flickering light would be the only thing touching her face, and with the softness of her long black hair laying on her silk pajamas she started with a down stroke across the strings, and in the rarest of female voices; contralto, like signing a bedtime story, she sang her song with a provocative smile that implied, "Hello world, I am introducing myself," and after completing her mesmerizing piece of sensuality, she posted it on YouTube.

Mandalay, Myanmar

Inside the core of Shwenandaw Monastery at sunrise – day of the full moon –

The five arrived to give food offerings –

They wrongfully assumed that their host, the gracious and eldest of the monks, to be serious and reflective about the stolen bone shards of Buddha, but this morning he had forgotten that lesson and shared through amusement and cynical teachings what he must have wanted to blurt out for weeks, "They stole two of our bone fragments." Joan pressed for answers, and he was happy to elaborate with specifics concerning the abbot monk from a competing temple who had arranged for the removal and disappearance of two pieces of bone, from what were then five pieces inside his shrine. With great certainty he blamed a start-up temple in another country with using his bone shards to gain credence and to increase attendance and entrance fees.

To the elder monk's delight; the five westerners were attentive and inquisitive, so he did the forbidden and allowed them to stroll freely among the younger monks who were sitting under trees seeking enlightenment. The monks, as young as thirteen, surrounded the tall white people and the questions started flying. This was the moment of two sides colliding, was it the snake and badger or was it to be the flower and hummingbird, there was no known protocol, but instincts warned the visitors to keep it simple as they were surely being watched and could be dismissed if they were too, too western.

The elder monk must have seen purity within their faces because he later rewarded the westerners with a sit-in during their morning meditation and chant. It was countless years ago when Leslie had last participated in a religious ceremony, but this morning she would allow herself some conformity and discipline, and with the hypnotic drumming she slipped into a pattern of self-examining thoughts; *I am nothing more than a self-organism which will fall into the eternity of time beyond the darken abyss without reincarnation, and for that I fear not. A creator makes no sense. I like window seats on these flights so I can look out onto villages of troubled souls of anguish crying with problems repeated, none of which will be important and will be forgotten in a few days. I am not troubled by questions, oh no, I have dissected life's purpose beyond any comprehension by fellow human. I could start my own deity and handle a mass following. I will turn my farm into an artist colony. These thoughts are racing through my head, need focus, maybe I should move and live here, my daughter needs to move out of my house, why is that dog over there licking his balls? Crud, I'm out of my trance.*

It took less than an hour for them to purchase guitars, bongo drums, a trumpet and harmonica, and get dropped off by tuk-tuk outside their hotel. During that short hour, Peter had also scrambled out lyrics about a young monk with a rice bowl and a gate between him and the sexy tuk-tuk driver that he dreamed to touch, that Burma backstreet girl that he had something to tell. The lyrics to "Don't Touch the Monks" were adventures that had been absorbed and needed to be sung - celibacy and I want to kick a ball. The Red Canal Resort & Spa had a grand piano located between the pool and the dining area where the five prepared their new equipment.

Leslie went to the piano and started harmonizing while Peter described a mood for her to adopt. It started as a mid-tempo piano solo until she was ready to develop it further, then it went to Nancy on the drum to create a baseline and her own solo, then to Joan and Catherine on guitar to split solos. They went into a free style jam until they each knew this moment was real, and then worked the melody to their monk song. They tried various tempos, always steadied by Nancy's drumming, and their early foundation was energy and fun. They refined

and blended their harmony with Peter signing his vocals until
they agreed it was infectious, and then they jammed unplugged
for another hour.

It was brought up that they needed a name, and while carrying their equipment three blocks away until reaching the entrance of Mandalay Palace, this fraction of Kentridge Class of
1980 decided to be called KR80 Tour.

The sum total of KR80 had found the fondness and trust
with each other that would allow the unveiling of their personalities as vulnerable artists to become the street musician
they each had begging to release from inside. To genuinely
play the part of street musicians they opened one guitar case
to catch even a minimal contribution, and they began by playing songs from well-known artists, with Leslie and Peter on
vocals. They were circled by enough tourists that it could be
defined as a crowd, and for the final epitaph of the evening
they performed their only song, which was a newborn from
earlier that same day, and paper money was dropped into the
guitar case.

Kingdom of Bhutan

A difficult country to gain entry by any tourist –

There was one question, followed by one frivolous answer.

"Are you all musicians?" asked Mr. Dorji, their assigned
tour guide.

"We're pretty famous back home," Peter answered.

Mr. Dorji loaded their equipment and luggage into his van
and whisked them away to their hotel, and from Peter's insin-
cere answer the destiny of KR80 was forever altered.

The afternoons of hiking and river rafting were completed when Mr. Dorji presented them with an offer that came
from the Director of National Tourism himself; the request
to musically perform on the third and final day of the King's
upcoming procession. A son was recently born to the young
king, so as traditional would have it; a procession was needed
in his honor.

KR80 would be provided with all the needed musical instruments, and they were to go electric, with amplifiers and a sound system fitting for the king's pleasure. There would be a violin added to the assorted mix of fun things to play with, as well as a drangyen, which they were asked to include with their playing. They each took a turn holding the foreign instrument that at least one of them would have to learn; a seven-string plucking instrument that they felt fit into the guitar family. They would be given unlimited rehearsal time and told that the king's ears were fond of the early Beatles songs.

There was another perplexing issue that Catherine asked of Mr. Dorji, "Why all the large penises?" As they had seen so many of them painted onto buildings, and other bright colored ornate erect penises carved out of wood and hanging from rooftops and doorways.

The answer from Mr. Dorji, "An age-old tradition of worshiping the phallus," provided them the hook for another lyric. It was agreed that they would compose an upbeat dance melody with a unique progression including backup vocals so all females sang the word 'penis' in the bridge. Mr. Dorji didn't object, so it progressed as a done deal.

Their rehearsals were some of their most bonding and fun hours together. They were cohesive in the goals and execution, and there was not an occasion when one member thought to correct another; they became a buffet of ideas that push and encouraged each other's creativity to come out.

Day one of the royal procession was just underway starting from a city on the western side of the country when Mr. Dorji came to them with yet another offer. The king himself had written a lyric and he hoped KR80 would turn it into a song that was to be played during the procession. They had two days to make that happen. It was also told to them that they would be granted what's forbidden to other tourists, a journey through the unlocked gates with access into the cave where Buddha had once meditated.

To ethos of the five were presented a scenario that could either embellish the tour or knock themselves down into an innocuous predicament. During lunch, Leslie had confessed she was carrying one chocolate edible bar, which she knew had a high concentrate of THC mixed in throughout, and proposed that they see Buddha's cave while in an altered state of mind. The group as a whole voted in the affirmative, and then they discussed the sacredness of the site in further details before re-voting to wait further into their journey before altering their consciousness.

KR80 were led by two guides up several steep hills and brought to the sacred shrine containing both a tooth relic from Buddha and a fragment from his skull. The squeaky steel doors were unlocked and they were advised to spend at least one hour inside the cave meditating, and told to "find and communicate with your animal spirit." The five found their seating spots deep enough inside the cave that only the slightest of light could penetrate, and like any untrained mind they waited in bewilderment and watched to see if someone else would teach them the process. It was Joan that "went away" first as she wanted to make peace with her damaged spirit and recalled whatever decisions she had made to date another man shortly before embarking on this tour. She didn't have conclusive evidence that her husband was unfaithful, only a premonition, but she dated that stranger three times and she had given him a fake name with an erroneous career; everything was a lie, including the house where he dropped her curbside, and it was exhilarating.

Their mediation was over and they shared their animal spirits with each other. Everyone saw piles of crawling snakes and was happy when they disappeared. There were also brown bears, but the strangest spirit animal appeared to Joan, who was the groups' germophobe, and that being a water buffalo on the opposite side of a large mud puddle that uncoiled its thirty foot long tongue to reach her arm and lick it with its sticky saliva. Peter was again scribbling his lyrics from this adventure.

KR80 was taken to the Great Hall inside Dunakha Dzong Temple where their instruments were arranged in their usual fashion, but the surprise went to Nancy, as they had furnished her with extra floor toms. "I'm going to go off. Try and keep up," she laughed to the others. It was at that moment when they all took notice of the camera crews setting up for Bhutan TV.

The procession was well in route and scheduled to arrive within ninety minutes, which gave them time to wander down the street to witness this royalist of events. At the lead point they saw dancers being followed by men swinging gold censers of burning incense, more people in ceremonial clothing, presumably those in higher office or those who had paid a contribution, followed by more people presenting embroidered banners, then the imperial umbrellas, and nearing was the queen with the baby both riding in a howdah atop the royal elephant, which was a change from the previous two days when they rode in a motor carriage. The queen was in her traveling wardrobe and her fly-whisk was in great swing when she approached KR80 roadside. The procession stopped momentarily because nobody in KR80 thought to bow, the only spectators not bowing, but they waved to the satisfaction of the queen, and the procession that was holding up the king not far behind was again moving forward.

It was Catherine who took to the drangyen and said to Peter, "You've got your own phrasing on our verse, and I'll jump in on the chorus," and off they went with their version of the king lyric, about his son growing into a great king, that was transformed into a tempo just daring the royal audience not to dance. In attendance was the Foreign Minister of India, sitting comfortably upfront and seemingly wanting to move his body more than he would like seen on television, so he did his best to play his dignified part of someone not easily influenced. Several songs into the evening they brought out the brass for the first time, and afterwards, Leslie performed a piano solo with a lyric about the king having a daughter, and how Leslie herself wanted to move here to be her friend, which was her antidote and her rebuttal to the king's masculinity. The meaning of her song was written with such ambiguity that the king couldn't have known that she was refuting him, but it certainly made herself feel better.

The foreign minister of neighboring India was the first to acknowledge them afterwards, and Peter intentionally let him know that Jaipur was to be their next destination. He told Peter that they would be met at the airport, and together they would widen the cultural bridge between Hinduism and western culture; plus he wanted to showcase their musical story while set in the beauty of India to promote tourism.

Jaipur, India

It would be their first paid gig. The Jesnaut Project is a four piece musical group of men, playing together since 2004 with several released instrumental singles, and they were traveling down from Delhi and sent KR80 the invitation to play alongside them at a big-time wedding ceremony joining two prominent families.

On the third morning of the ceremony, the actual day of the wedding, they were chauffeured to the bride's home, which was a house of many rooms in spectacular opulence and colorful decorations, and it was in the private garden where they first met the members of The Jesnaut Project, and although the-five were there on merit and invitation they politely ingratiated themselves to their host band with flattery and awe.

It was Leslie's dexterity that would be challenged as she would need her fingers to adapt to the keyboard presented her as she was informed that the tones fit better than piano with classical Indian music. The Jesnaut Project was a band of sitars and tabla (bongo drums) that played ancient Hindu sounds, but without vocals. The morning rehearsal started with guitar licks bouncing off sitar licks that evolved into a tug of two cultures searching for the escaping harmony that was hiding on the back side of two darkening worlds, so after an extended morning jam session, it was agreed that they would not coalesce into one, but rather they would take the stage as two opposing bands playing at separate moments. The audience would hear a composition of classical Indian sounds before someone in KR80 would blend-in to steal the moment away towards a western rock sound, and the process would repeat like a fencer dropping their sword and bowing to a newer and more hypnotic beauty.

It was midnight and many of the four hundred or so guests were still dancing to his music. It would later be said by Peter, a man who cannot dance and has makes his income by producing fictitious newsreels, that the satisfaction and the thrill of creating something real that induced other people dance was to him the highlight of not only the ceremony but the journey to that point.

Om was sipping his first taste of beer in many years. He sat alone at any one of the many outdoor cafes and he was halfway gone from leaving his family forever, especially and specifically his four daughters, them little bitches.

Funneling from the adjacent street bazaar were five blissful Americas dressed in new Hindu clothing and looking for lunch, and it was Catherine who asked Om if he minded sharing his table, as everything else was already occupied.

As they soon learned from Om, he was, before this morning, a Pujari, a Hindu temple priest, who woke up to four daughters complaining, and he felt finished. Leslie, who was all too familiar with battles of estrogen rage in her domain, took the lead at calming this pillar of a father with stories of her daughter. Then they were laughing.

Pujari Om drove them three hills out of town and into a valley to where the road ended. They followed him on a walking path through reeds and cattails towering as high as their heads to a clearing of lotus before a stone temple, as small as a one room house, and not listed on any tourist map.

The diarist Nancy wrote of this experience, "Om showed us three skullcups, each from a human skull, none of which he personally knew. One was mounted with jewels, another had a carving on top imaged as a dancing skeleton strumming a sitar, and the one he used for us was decorated with silver. He turned it upside down like a bowl and filled it with wine and he gave it a priests' blessing. He instructed us to hold it in our left hand only and to start drinking, and Peter went first, then the skull cap was passed around the room. I did it without thinking much. Joan was last and cautiously hesitant. He explained the ritual, as we continued with more sips, that it was a symbol of wisdom that will lead us to enlightenment and a higher state of consciousness. We kept passing that cranium around drinking and drinking until the skull was empty and dry. We then prepared ourselves for meditation and suddenly an afternoon monsoon shock and drenched our sky, it was the timing that made it weird. Maybe it was fifteen minutes into the meditation when I saw myself as a teenager standing atop a mound of dirt that was centered in a sprawling cow pasture circled by a mote of mosquito infected still water. What was most amazing was while talking with the others afterwards; they too saw themselves as that same girl, even Peter. Catherine said she was that teenage girl and wearing a vibrant bright blue silk dress and inhaling smoke from a burnt brush pile still smoldering from yesterday. Leslie was a bit freakish; she said that she was that girl on the mound holding a shepherd's crook and happily thrilled that her breasts were finally growing but also anguished that there was nobody and nowhere to show them off. Joan asked of Om why she saw it too and added that she felt herself breathing in the smoky air as well, and that she was illiterate and hoped to get married. So Om gave us the answer - that we obtained knowledge from the person to whom the skull had belonged.

Catherine, Joan and Nancy had a rhythm arranged to a new song later that afternoon. It was the first time that a melody was created before Peter and Leslie had completed the lyrics. They went with a slow soulful blues sound, and called it Monsoon Flower Daughter. That evening, the guests at Hotel Jas Vilas were treated to session by the pool of KR80 fine tuning their harmonies.

Amber Fort, a lavish palace that housed rulers as far back as the 16th century, was selected by several ministers from the Indian government as the most treasured and visually pleasing site in Jaipur in which to display the wonders and colors of India during the upcoming concert. The stage was set in the shadows of the inner courtyard, large enough to hold a football field, and an acoustic dream that would swirl the best of ambient sounds.

It was sunset on June 24, 2017 with the courtyard packed with people lying on blankets when Peter walked on stage carrying a large conch shell, followed by his classmates and The Jesnaut Project. The concert was a live televised event shown throughout India and Sri Lanka. Peter blew the conch shell like a trumpet to destroy any disease-causing germs lingering in the atmosphere; a Hindu custom, and then he blew it twice more to make sure he got it all.

Creations were fed from Nancy's tight drum beats that were a soulful blues and sharp staccato sounds from her snares, which led to tormented vocals of passion for the lost soul of the Monsoon Flower Daughter in a duet of Leslie and Peter with lyrics about tripping over daughters and nurturing them back, then to squish them and water them again. *Gravity is all we agree on, daughter, our course is a blurry confusion.* The keyboard played by Leslie was a sweet element that led into The Jesnaut Project caressing the air with sounds rooted in Hindu traditions and familiar to the audience. The first song had the only vocals of the evening, and when the musicianship returned to KR80 they laid out stinging sound of domineering guitar work in up tempo crisp-tight reggae rhythms then demonstrating their prowess they eased back down to a bridge of slow blues beats. For two hours they continued improvising and creating new sounds and were out-performing The Jesnaut Project, who were squirming and unable to play outside their confines.

Peter thanked the audience for their spiritual awakening, for being such wonderful hosts, he even thanked them for turning him onto Butter Chicken, that they would always remember looking up at the sky with the hundreds of kites flown from rooftops, and the incredible colors that were cemented into his head, and he announced that they were traveling onto Tanzania.

Tanzania, East Africa

For two afternoons they did a bush-walk into the Serengeti National Park and for two evenings they played their music from atop one of the three wooden observation decks overlooking the Serengeti. The center observation deck was reserved for their playing; it was the largest of the three and had electrical hook-up, it was open-air with a wood roof providing shade and it was accessed by a bridge as it was easily twenty-feet above ground offering protection from wild straying predators. For the other guests, it was accepted as a fair trade off to surrender one deck in exchange for evening music to compliment the amazing views.

On the edge of the Serengeti sits Buckman Reserve, an upscale resort in its inaugural year, and where co-owner Rolf Stöhr spent much of the past two days like a peacock spreading his colorful feathers, trying to win the affection of Joan, until the third evening when she finally acquiesced to dinner, but her terms were that if only the whole group was invited would she agree.

The five arrived for dinner and Joan was outfitted in a sexy white dress and sat next to Rolf while he explained that in the morning he was leading an overnight expedition with two vehicles through the Serengeti and camping in the Olduvai Gorge, and he encouraged the group to join him. He told them about a small team of French archeologists that were digging in the gorge and discovering bones and tools from early man, and that this specific gorge, with high probability, is the place where it all started for us, where early man originated, and where a skull was recently discovered from 1.7 million years ago.

There would be one other group down in the gorge that they would also encounter, the Sorens, a group of men with the self-destiny of launching a new religion that they aspired to not only rival Christianity and Islam throughout the African continent, but to replace them altogether.

It was Joan and Rolf that hiked up the gorge to meet with the Sorens and to learn further of their endeavors. There was a leader with sixteen prophets, which he routinely sent out to live and meditate within the gorge and report back to him of their visions, which he then recorded into his book as written records that were to be the foundation to making the Sorens beliefs available to the masses throughout the continent.

They believed with absolute surety that there was a prophet to God that ascended to the heavens before Mohammad and even before Christ, and the tangible link that they needed to prove it was somewhere very close to them, but still buried within the gorge. With conviction he laid out their beliefs for their monotheistic religion and how they would employ objects and create ceremonies with rituals and symbols, but it needed to be centrally based from the African continent; in fact, it was disturbing to him that no major religion had originated from Africa. He said to them that he had other teams that were right now creating sites throughout Africa that would be of historical importance to Sorens, and other needed sites that would be shrouded in mystery. They were still working on their name for God, and when that was settled and their book was completed, it would be presented at the Assembly of the African Union to be adopted and sold as the new native religion by all states in a leap forward for social and economic stability. Joan was enlightened at how simple starting a new religion appeared to be, just 1,2,3, steps. She suggested to the leader that divine punishment should be omitted, but he disagreed and said it was essential.

While Peter sat listening to Rolf tell them further about the expedition, he was finding it amusing to watch Joan, an intelligent woman flirting and processing all her possibilities.

Rolf had also invited and added to the expedition a traditional healer from the Maasai tribe. He explained how the healer was a conduit between the living and their deceased relatives, should they need to connect with them for instruction on how to resolve various concerns and family dilemmas.

While Joan and Rolf were away talking with the Sorens, and shortly before sunset, Peter entered the tent of the healer and asked him to connect with his deceased son in order to find out if his expensive mountain bike was truly stolen from their garage, as his son had sworn it was years earlier. The healer clapped his hands then pulled from a bag several hyena bones and tossed them like dice onto his floor mat. He said that his son would be in control of how the bones would lie for him to read. The healer told Peter, "He sold your bike while you were out of town, and he is sorry."

Catherine entered the tent of the healer. Her grandmother and mother had both died with Alzheimer's disease. She wanted them to tell her if she would also get Alzheimer's. The healer clapped his hands and tossed out bone fragments from an antler onto the floor. "Yes, you will not recognize your husband or your children and you will forget all from this journey."

Leslie asked advice from her grandfather if she should sell her business now or wait 'til later. The healer threw anteater bones and translated the advice, "Do not sell. Your daughter will take it in a good direction."

Nancy was wearing her deceased grandmother's earrings and wanted to know if her youngest brother should go on his trip to South America and leave his terrible girlfriend behind. The healer tossed out numerous animal vertebrae bones along with the earrings to the floor. The healer had long discussions with the grandmother before translating, "Tell your brother that he must go very soon, and to go alone."

While sitting around campfire and surrounded by the buried bones of early man, the question and topic from Peter was, "Have we done it right for ourselves?"

Catherine was the quickest with, "No. We were given a perfect world from our creator and we don't appreciate the gift that was given to us. I mean, we ignore our relationship with him and we show him how we don't need him."

Joan added, "Well, I think we have done well with medicine, and extending our life expectancy."

"I don't agree that longer life is the answer or the solution. I think we should improve the quality of our lives with more travel, and increasing our family time would be the improvement I believe in," Leslie said.

Nancy added, "Overall, no, we deceive each other too much for benefit."

"Could we have done it better?" Peter asked.

After much debate that it's innate in humans to better ourselves, making war and struggle unavoidable, it was unanimously agreed that humans did it right, except for currency, which led us on a bad path, and those people that predict the end of the world, we could certainly do without them, and whoever was that group which allowed the first person to become their leader, they really screwed it up too, and it was agreed that males and females did a remarkable job of bringing each other along and holding each other up, and it was also agreed that civilization depends on too much technology.

It was exactly 10pm and the fire was kicked and its light stamped out in preparation for 10:07pm, when they all looked up to the eastern sky and watched the International Space Station flying westward over them at over 15,000 mile per hour.

To lay witness to that achievement from the same area where early man began had left them uncertain about their preceding beliefs.

Earlier that same evening, around dinner time at the fire pit, Rolf had been talking about the five teenage boys from the Maasai tribe that would be riding along for the expedition once it resumed in the morning. Each of those five teenagers had come of age and had started on their rite-of-passage to manhood, but next, as tradition dictated, they needed to kill a lion, and then get circumcised, which were all as part of the process to manhood. The five teenagers had been dropped off at the rim of the canyon, earlier in the day, in order to scout for a male lion and surround it before each throwing their long spears into its ribcage for the kill. Unfortunately, they had been unsuccessful at finding any lions, and consequently they had met the group around the fire pit earlier that evening and were feeling defeated.

Rolf was a driver and the armed ranger when they drove out in the morning looking for a masculine lion, which would turn those boys into warriors, and perhaps he was taking extra risks by driving further off path than normal and approaching very close to a particular blind spot around the granite kopjes, as even he was getting spooked, but he knew the importance of the process to manhood so certainly he would push their safety a little more than usual.

He told the group not to stand up or to make any noises, for he himself had sensed some irritation was brewing in the grassy plains nearby. His instincts told him to speed up, but it was too late as a male lion was reaching full speed under an acacia tree but a hundred feet away and closing on them. Their safari vehicle was open-sided and offered no protection. The five Maasai teenagers, sitting in the other vehicle, each sprang to their feet in fear and preparation to heave their spears when the range was right, and the range was right just now as five spears with metal tips all landed short of their target as they had no experience from throwing but on still ground. Catherine, whom years earlier was an unarmed victim of a violent home invasion, would not let it happen again, and grabbed the rifle from Rolf's side and flipped the safety off shooting three consecutive bullets with at least enough of them bringing the lion down fifteen feet short of the rear bumper. A sense of collective stoicism settled in the group as no other lions appeared on the horizon. Peter grabbed his breath and a pen to write down everything he could remember screaming out of Catherine's mouth all aimed at Rolf releasing her anger that they had to kill. Peter himself let the raging go on without contribution as he thought shooting the lion was the most auspicious act to ensure there would be another dinner time and another sunrise. Peter, while still riding in the safari vehicle, penciled these verses; "Answers from the Serengeti."

Your reign on the plain
up top the chain
Freshly stirring my mind
You inspired this time
The winds changed and things were arranged
Let me tell
your story bloody well
we should sit on a rock
Top the chains, poisons to unlock
The winds changed and things were arranged
Left back right or lost
Too tired will be the cost
My tracks a smell can't decimate
Running over flies for the gate
The winds changed and things were arranged
You're closing fast no hesitates
Hide pauses to fears of eviscerates
She's tasting eternal evaporates
Spinning harrowing time 'n fates
The winds changed and things were arranged
Our maze is quiet less one be free
Comin' fully the misery
Your pride and not me
Milking the jasmine air I seed
Blinding the burning steel you bleed
Thinning the herds we do it too
I prowled at night just like you

Back two nights earlier, and while at dinner with Rolf and Joan in her white sexy dress and about the time they were agreeing to join that expedition, Rolf had asked them if he could record them playing out on his observation deck into an album and to use it as a hotel promotion, and that he would invite Level Play Records to produce it professionally. "All good friends of mine," he told them.

They rushed back from the kill, full of emotions, and went right to their instruments to work out their anger. Level Play Records was set up, and under orders from the band, were advised not to interrupt.

There was a need to feel raw with nature so nothing but bikini swimsuits were worn and Peter would express himself wearing only shorts. He said to Joan, "Give us your riff of how you feel and we'll take off from there." They found a melody and Peter worked in his new verses. They turned on the pedals, the chords progressed, and Peter looked out onto the plains and saw a tower of giraffes walking their way. As the music progressed they were emotionally going off and playing harder than they ever had before; they couldn't contain their nerves and started jumping up and down. Peter felt he was bestowed a trust that these four women, which he had all known since third-grade, would strip down to the bare of their bikinis and present a vestige of their animal souls in front of him. He also wondered how long it had been since either of their husbands had seen their wives so turned on, so excited, and so involved; he was mesmerized by the belly-dance circles from their hips; everywhere those hips have been and now they are with me. At the point when their music reached its crescendo of cohesive magnitude a giraffe stuck its head and upper neck over the railing of the observation deck and paused its ear next to Peter's, who was in full vocals, and didn't flinch. The giraffe and Peter swayed together and Peter wrapped his arm around its head while singing, and when the beat would pick back up the giraffe would sway with such a whip that Peter had to duck his head so not to be clobbered. Joan would later share that she had a sense of loneliness during that recording as she wouldn't believe that they could ever again capture that emotion and intensity.

"We had found freedom. We weren't dedicated to any case. There was no rebellion. We weren't trying to build anything, and we could be profoundly cynical, because we could get on a plane and simply fly home anytime we chose," she added.

Months earlier while structuring and finessing the travel itinerary, there was genuine overall trepidation about Egypt and for their safety, should they chose to explore there; why with the unrest since the 2011 uprising and arbitrary arrests for debauchery and immorality, they had good cause for concern, but it was finally agreed that they would see a couple of pyramids and quickly fly out.

Cairo, Egypt

They started shortly after 7 o'clock in the evening with Catherine on a lute, then Joan on a flute, then three guitars, all playing their newest song while inside the King's Chamber of the Great Pyramid of Khufu. They had arranged their candles around the large granite sarcophagus; they had carried in their own instruments up the steep narrow passageway, and from the hour earlier, the Giza Plateau had been closed to tourism.

They had each been filmed, outside the Egyptian Museum, with convincing fervent speeches using candid words to convince the outside world that they were safe and treated well here in Cairo. The film crew then took them to the Khan el-Khalili Bazaar, where they were shown walking amongst friendly shop keepers and negotiating fair deals on souvenirs.

The afternoon prior, the group was off on their own and looking at a large stone wall of hieroglyphs and listening to a small group of teenage boys laughing while one of them was interpreting its meaning.

Nancy asked the one that was doing the interpreting, "Why is that funny. What does it say?"

"There once was a priest that would tell a man whether or not to marry his woman. First, garlic was pushed into his woman's vagina, and then wait a day, the priest would smell into her mouth. If he could smell garlic it was good for the man because he could know that she could make babies. No garlic, then her body was blocking and no babies," he explained.

The group that was a car full of teenage boys and KR80 found each other amusing and was a serendipitous encounter of musicians traveling to the Red Pyramid, which happens to be located further out of town than most other pyramids and thus generally uncrowded, and on this particular afternoon the parking area was empty, giving them uninterrupted access through the two-hundred feet of passageway and solidarity inside the third chamber. The teenage boys were Muslim, so the use of musical instruments was unlawful, and they were further limited by only being permitting to sing as a cappella. Both groups fanned out against the red limestone walls in a room that is similar in size to an average living-room, and the boys in tenor voices sang a verse, then they paused for the Americans to mimic what they had just heard, and for a blissful episode, each singer had mastered and was able to hold their pitch. They continued for three songs about Islamic beliefs and history before switching to western folksongs. It seemed oddly reckless to the Americans that the boys were filming his harmonious moment onto their phones as laws were being broken. It was Joan that told her group after leaving the pyramid, "If we get into the Great Pyramid, I think a flute would sound perfect."

Peter had a message on his cell phone from Mr. Rashed, which made it his fourth overall call to Peter, and who was negotiating on their behalf, "I have approval your twenty-minutes inside the King's Chamber and with one instrument only, which must be a lute."

Tucked away inside Joan's backpack resting against the sarcophagus and hidden under extra candles were two teeth. During the morning before the Red Pyramid, they had ridden a boat four miles up the Nile, and following their hiking guide book, departed at Wadi Degla.

Perhaps they hiked further into the rolling desert hills than their guide book recommended, but around noon they came upon two girls selling their bracelets and other handcrafted wares to the few that would venture in far enough to find them, and the Nubian village in which they lived in. They saw goats and camels and one girl asked them, "Are you Americans?" Nancy confirmed and they were told, "Come with us, my father will want to meet you."

They were led to an open fire pit next to a three large tents tied together as one and were offered mint tea to drink. They were brought inside and met a man of advanced age and by appearances not far off from his own death. The girls translated when the old man tapped on a small tin container already opened, which was holding two teeth, each lying on a cloth, "These are teeth from Mohamad the creator of Islam."

The tin was handed to Peter and the old man spoke to his girls, and the story will be shared, "Mohamad was in a war when he was struck by a metal weapon that knocked-out four of his teeth. Two are in Turkey, and these two left from Mecca with Ethiopian warriors returning from battle, and they brought them over the Red Sea in the 7th century, and through trade our father has them."

While the teeth were rolled with fingertips, the girl continued, "these were revered relics until the reforms during the 18th century when Islam condemned such worshipping as idolatry, so it's been forbidden for us to cherish these, and it's been a secret that he has them."

Peter hands the tin back to the old man, who pushes back insisting that Peter keep them. "We cannot do anything with them, and if we showed someone local, they would take them and make a big problem for us," the girl says.

Joan asked her friends to huddle around as she explained, "My husband does DNA recovery and analysis, and he'll know how to handle this."

Peter handed her the tin, "If those are legitimate, I propose we make a group decision on what's best to do with them," and his proposal was agreed to.

Their new song; the one they started playing inside of the King's Chamber, began with lyrics created from both Catherine and Leslie, who both valued a good morning of sleeping-in, and who were both terribly irritated over their first night in Cairo, when the Call to Prayer hit the speakers at 4am, and didn't relent for an hour keeping them awake. They had both stood on their hotel balcony trying to pin-point the origin of this catastrophe. They have since learned that the origin came from several locations among the many Minarets and Mosques within their eyesight. There was nobody for them to call and complain, nobody to negotiate a better deal with, thus, sleeping past 4am was, unrealistic.

At sunrise and during breakfast, they became a cohort of two pissed-off artists working the metaphorical lyrics of "Shooting those Speakers with a Rifle," which would be their only source of satisfaction against this intolerable loss of justice.

It was also during that same breakfast when Mr. Rashed, the Minister of Tourism, found them at their table in the back courtyard of the Marriott Cairo & Omar Khayyam Casino, and pitched to them his first request, "I would like the five of you to act in a promotion video covering tourist safety in Egypt." He went on to explain that they were the perfect look, so genuine, and using models wouldn't be as authentic.

It was Nancy who envisioned the perfect tradeoff, "put us inside the Great Pyramid to play our music." Even the rest of her friends were stunned by that boldness and yet idyllic proposal.

Mr. Rashed thought it through and responded, "That's not possible. Maybe in front of the pyramid it would work."

"Nope, how prosaic, how blah, but playing inside the pyramid, I'm sure that's never been done before," Nancy responded with intensity.

"The Muslim Brotherhood would first, never agree to men and women singing together, and certainly no instruments, and plus, I'd have to satisfy the Minister of Antiquities. Being up in the pyramid, I don't think so."

It was just the evening before meeting Mr. Rashed for the first time, while they were passing through Customs at the airport, that the five were detained, and besides being asked which hotel they were staying, there also seemed to be extra questioning and from extra officials, because unknown to them at that time, they were being auditioned by the authorities.

Yerevan, capital of Armenia

And first nation to adopt Christianity as a state religion; 301AD –

This newly intriguing tourist hot-spot has been victorious, as well as defeated, in many battles with each of its neighbors starting back at a period before Christ and continuing through today, with cease-fire violation and mortar attacks on civilians, and to say that every empire has once fought to take control of this tiny nation would barely be an overstatement.

Parliamentary elections were freshly concluding at the time that KR80 arrived, and with general rejection for the results, there were mass arrests, there was violence acted against journalists and random stabbing of civilians, and to say that the atmosphere was yeasting a riot with the city disintegrating into chaos was not an overstatement.

Months earlier before their arrival, they had sent away for opening night tickets to Puccini's La Boheme at the Armenian Opera House, which was now four days away, but Catherine had just finished reading a local clip about Sosi Simonian, who was to be one of the starring opera singers, and arrested the night before for a bribery scandal in which she had offered 1,000 euros cash to an Opera Critic in exchanged for an outstanding review describing her as the next generation of operetta superstars.

The problem for Sosi Simonian, besides currently being under house arrest, was that the Opera Critic had reached inside his pants pocket and was recording her bribery with the offer that he should remove the brown envelope from her purse if he accepted.

Catherine, born Catherine Kataroyan of Armenian descent, felt a connection with the heritage, and with an impulse to fill the gap she went straight to the opera house to convince the director that she could sing the part, and it is now known that the director was captivated by her operetta voice and her high aptitude for learning; plus he was excited to replace the usual Soprano voice with Catherine's Contralto voice. She would fill-in on opening night, which gave the director another week to secure a permanent replacement.

With Catherine at her rehearsals, the other four went to visit the oldest Christian church in existence anywhere in the world, Etchmiadzin Cathedral, and upon entering they heard Gregorian music and saw a ceiling so high that every sound echoed as the big wooden door slammed loudly behind them, and there was Deacon Tateossian, busying himself with chores, and who was shocked to have a tourist on such a tense day as he was relocating his most important relic to a safer location in case the riots and vandalism were to reach his church. Deacon Tateossian had in his hands The Holy Lance while he invited them to sit with him and discuss their issues. Leslie sat next to him and immediately felt ensconced in his presence as if he had swirled a net of rapture around her. He was warm but laconic with his words and Leslie slid further into a spell of joy and servitude towards him. She wanted him to continue talking with his soothing voice and she yearned for him to touch her arm or a shoulder to complete a needed physical connection, as she wondered, "Would all the worries disappear in marrying a man of the cloth?" The Deacon was telling the other three that were still listening of the twelve inch long metal spear head that he was holding in his hands as probably the most important and venerated early Christian relic in the world, it was right up there with Jesus' circumcised foreskin and The Holy Grail.

Nancy asked, "What is it for?"

"This is the spear tip that the Roman soldier used during the crucifixion to pierce the side of Jesus while he hung on the cross to ensure a death."

"Wow, how did you get it?" Joan asked.

"St. Thaddeus, he was one of the twelve apostles at The Last Supper. He came to Armenia to introduce Christianity and he carried it with him."

Released from her trance, Leslie asked, "So this made Jesus suffer?"

"No, he was already dead."

"Why was it that Christians were so willing to suffer at the hands of those who hated them? I mean, why didn't they fight back?" Leslie asked.

"Suffering will bring you closer to God, and to face prosecution at the hands of pagan hostilities, what a great way for the truth to be known."

The Deacon then made the rarest and unexpected reward to Leslie, "Would you like to carry this into the basement for me?"

While Leslie was carrying The Holy Lance down ancient spiral stone steps, she pushed her fingertip into the tip of spear, and then Joan reached over her shoulder and pushed her fingertip in as well, and Peter and Nancy got their fingers in it too, done swiftly before the Deacon could notice.

Once outside that church, they described a sublime cinnamon perfume scent ascending from their hands.

With the Red Army encircling their city in the final days of World War II, many of the German elite class attended the Berlin Philharmonic in blackout and applauded in standing ovation with a lack of apathy for the oncoming air raids –

Tonight in Yerevan the trains and buses were on strike, the international airport was closed, three of the most popular tourist areas in the center of town; Republic Square, Old Brick Theatre, and Swan Lake Park, were all too dangerous to enter, and lock-downs and curfews were the buzz on the streets –

Catherine first appeared on stage in Act 2 while entering a Parisian cafe. She was elegantly dressed and commanding, and is followed by an aging boyfriend whom she has lost interest in. She is playing the part of the sly Musetta, who has drifted between many other lovers and crushed each of their hearts. Once inside the cafe she spots one such former lover and confidently and radiantly launches loudly into a risqué song about her own beauty and how people passionately desire her, which is her attempt to rekindle their lost love before Catherine falls into his embracing arms. In Act 3, that same lover has tired of Catherine's flirtatious nature as the two sing an arguing duet that becomes a violent quarrel, and to this point Catherine has executed her role with panache. During the final Act she transpires to a more introspective and benevolent soul while comforting a girlfriend to her death, which stirred and captivated the packed house of 1,400 through her very last operatic note.

The after-opera party was canceled for security reasons, and it was around 11:30, Catherine still in a glowing high of excitement that she had pulled it-off, and Peter trying to lead them a safe route back to their hotel, when suddenly insults were barraged at them from a man in a passing car. The five were formally dressed foreigners, and maybe he saw them as upper-class no-gooders and viable targets, but he quickly braked to a halt and thrust himself from his car into a warring posture, and with insults escalating he was face-to-face with them, an aggression that was a contingency to a brawl being inevitable.

It was Leslie, who was still trying to figure out what accepting suffering really meant, who chose to let him act his pagan hatred on her and found the courage to say, "Please forgive me," which only excited the rage from the man, and with a group of youths encircling the battle, she realized that loving this man and suffering from his hand would offer no benefits, so like a turbulent wind she was in his driver's seat and locking the door. Her four friends were inside the car before she shifted into first and sped off. They had commandeered his car, they had rolled the windows down to laugh at the fool, and they threw his cell phone out onto the street.

Peter ordered up several bottles of wine and they gathered in Nancy's room to play guitar and wait for Catherine to unwind from her performance. They mutually agreed that running to the U.S. Consulate to escape the riots would effectively end their trip, so that was not a worthwhile option, however, they did agree that they needed to get out of town, but just how, well, that solution was still needed. Catherine's husband called to inquire about joining the trip, which was left undecided because she was too intoxicated to focus, and she switched subjects by interrupting him with, "This is my song," and began singing to him.

Joan's husband called to see about his options in coming over, which was cut short because she had drunk too much of the truth serum and couldn't articulate a lucid sentence beyond, "I'm not drunk and I have to tell you all a secret."

With no sleep at 4:30 that morning it was Leslie that said, "I have the best idea! Let's find us a plane," and they soon drove away from Ibis Center hotel, using their stolen car, to a small aviation airport located thirty minutes SE of the city, and began looking for an airplane to steal.

Nobody would later remember his mumbling, but Peter was determined that they needed to lift-off at the moment of sunrise. There was no activity at the airport, nobody working in the tower, no maintenance crew, no other pilots, just the five of them walking near the tarmac in search of the best thing with wings and propeller, so it would be chosen according to Peter. About one-hundred yards out from the hanger he settled on a ten seat dual-engine and broke its door lock. He flipped a few switches and checked for fuel while Nancy spread out her regional hikers map onto the floor of the cabin. That map illustrated mountain regions with lakes and rivers and would be their navigational tool, because Peter would not be turning on any of the radio equipment as they needed to stay covert. They lifted off and headed straight north, and estimated at adjusting their course at five degrees to the east to the direction of their destination. Leslie sat in the copilot seat and called out landmarks, which the other three in the back could use to pinpoint on their map and needed adjustments were called forward, "Stay five miles left of that lake," and "Split that mountain up the middle." In a half hour, if everything went as planned, they would be over the border and a half hour more they could land somewhere near Tbilisi, the capital city of Georgia.

Tbilisi, Georgia

They flew undetected over the Caucuses and found a roadway which guided them in. It was navigated by others and interpreted to Peter, "You want that valley," and flying low like a crop duster he banked sharply to make the adjustment and looked back to see Nancy enjoying the champagne that she had been carrying, and wearing a content face of someone no longer afraid to die.

Peter saw train tracks that appeared to be going east into the city and with its train far enough out, he was able to alert his crew, "We want that train." They descended into a flat agricultural area that they surmised as a wine grape region and Peter sat it down on a rural paved road without being witnessed because not even a farmer was working just yet. They had landed near the small town of Telavi and turned into the parking lot of Shalauri Wine Cellars where they quickly abandoned the plane.

It was to be the simple routine act of a tractor blade cutting underneath a layer of grass in preparation of soil to rows of plowed farmland, when suddenly that blade tugged and stalled and hooked onto an ancient mud and brick wall buried just below the surface of the dirt. The plower, a woman, dug deeper to discover two long handled copper spoons, and using a corner edge of her tractor blade she went deeper until the sun's reflection showed her several steel tools, some were sharp and probably used for engraving, and one was a bronze dagger, and another foot deeper she unearthed a female human skeleton, minus the skull, along with handheld stone and bone carving tools, and at that same level she was able to see several pieces of broken pottery. The hole which she had just dug was large enough that she could confirm that the remains of the circular brick wall was in fact the bottom half of an existing structure which featured a painting of one anthropomorphic happy female figurine sitting at the side of one large Kvevri ceramic pot, which in itself was three feet high and egg-shaped, and decorated near the top with etchings of grape clusters. She was Claudia Buchsbaum, land owner and first-time farmer and future hopeful winemaker, and she was all too familiar with that style of terracotta pottery, as it was used thousands of years ago to ferment wine, just as the pots are still used today. A sickening and disastrous feeling overwhelmed Claudia as she abandoned the treasures in that open pit, and while she relocated her tractor to the opposite side of her property.

That tractor blade would soon thrust the five friends into a debate over erroneously altering a little slice of ancient history, and if by doing so it would place a thick wad of currency into some pockets.

The morning, before that debate would begin, got underway during breakfast when Nancy described to the others that something had happened the previous evening during their two-hour guided walking tour of historical Tbilisi. She told them about two reoccurring and frustrating dreams; one being that she is passed a soccer ball during a game and at the moment of receiving the ball her muscles seize and become immobilized making her unable to kick the ball into the goal, and her second dream is about standing in front of two white-painted double doors with a wiggly-loose turn handle. She confides at this time, that among other issues, she has seen a therapist to unlock the meaning of these dreams, but she had left each session without any resolute understanding, so she later tried hypnosis, which was also of no avail. She goes on to tell that last night's tour had brought them past those double doors from her dream, and that there was a homeless man sitting in front counting his dirty handful of coins, which was identical in that an odd person always blocks the doorway in her dreams. She goes on to describe how she had frozen with curiosity but the premonition to finally discover the content of the unknown was too much for her to handle last night, so she lost her confidence and simply followed the tour away. Nancy was so bothered that she hadn't conquered that one mystery space yet unexplored, that she was now going back alone to push through.

The other four were two hours on Khorakert trail hiking through lush hills and over pristine creeks and occasionally stopping to catch a look at the few parasailers overhead, when at the point they reached a trail sign that it was still 15km to their destination, Catherine in the lead, and without a spoken word to the others, started jogging and sensed they would join and keep pace. It was a beautiful taste of life to each challenge themselves that this endeavor could be conquered and they were alive enough to keep it going, and keeping it going for several miles they did, until the trail passed Claudia's little wooden hut café, where she sold her version of apple strudel and iced tea.

Claudia would confide in them her worrisome quandary. She had recently purchased the nine hectares of land sitting adjacent to her little hut, with its fertile soil, ideal for growing wine grapes, and they looked out onto her property and they could tell that she had already cultivated about a quarter of her twenty-two acres. She gets to the sticky points, "The families around here, that already own vineyards, tried to stop me because I'm a woman. The little shits, they're trying to pass new law that only families rooted here from over one-hundred years can farm land, and when they check my ancestry, shit, my family came here three generation before from Israel. Two parasailers were preparing to land on her farm, "That happens every day," she said.

They followed Claudia to the pit where the treasures lie and where she tells them that she needs to finish plowing in order get the start-up vines planted within a month, or else she would have to wait another year, but now she has this dilemma in her way, and if she shows this to an archeologist or tells the imperious Minister of Monument Protection, and she tells them that's a real positon because of all the archeology digs nearby, then she's going to have her land taken away, and no matter what she does, her loans for the land and the tractor won't just go away.

"I read that the first winemaking started here eight-thousand years ago. Is that true?" Catherine asked.

"Yes, just in the next valley over," Claudia confirms and goes into the pit to claim a hand size piece of broken pottery, "They used big pottery pots to ferment the grapes, and this is a piece from such a pot."

That piece of pottery was priority-mail overnighted to Joan's husband for chemical analysis.

While Claudia was seeking advice on backfilling over an ancient settlement and getting her plants in the ground, or to let officials confiscate her land for years of digging, Nancy had stepped around a mumbling old barefoot woman who on any other day would have received a greeting and a touch on her shoulder, but this moment couldn't afford distractions, she finally swung open those doors and inhaled a poignant dose of balsamic smelling cedarwood that reminded her of a dark moment long in her past, that moment of self-doubt that her promiscuous lifestyle had destroyed any chance of a glorious future, but today standing in that corridor of cedarwood she felt levitated above any norm of comfort and routine, and with her realization that she's easily bored and relationships just take too much damn work, so she would continue walking into the path of unpredictable, to be impulsive and stimulated by temptation and to pull her pants down in the moonlight whenever she desired. "I will not allow this torture into the equation of my life any longer," she thought. "Fuck that," she said out loud and entered another door to the workshop of Dado Mamedov, and to her eyes, the luscious Dado, who was working his underground enterprise in stolen relics, missing relics, and the few certified relics. Dado would leave work early that day for a rendezvous of drinks with Nancy, who was already enjoying the excitement that comes with a ten-day fling.

Two close-up pictures of the Oosik arrived to Nancy's phone, both sent from her youngest brother, Koda, with the text message, "look at the notches and carvings. Do you remember the tales that both our uncles used to tell us? I think this is it."

III

When I first interviewed Koda Deschene over his relevance to the Oosik, he wanted me to capture the essence as a man blindly drunk but rising to the occasion just at the final moment of her greatest despair, and her being a beautiful woman in distress. When I interviewed him eye-to-eye, he didn't know if Interpol had an interest in his whereabouts or if his safety was in jeopardy; either way, his circumstances were his excuse to play-out his motto, "I am at my best when I'm in motion."

Koda wanted his story with the Oosik to begin on the afternoon in which he had just departed from a Malbec wine tasting tour in Mendoza, Argentina. He was soon flying over the Andes with the dark fruit and smoky tastes still fresh on his tongue to a short layover in Santiago, Chile before his flight north to Calama, where he planned to explore the Atacama Desert, which happens to be the driest place on earth. Koda was, and maybe still is, a longtime resident and bachelor from Idaho fervently doing the last purpose he has left to care about: traveling alone on vacation to add thrilling experiences into his repertoire.

Town of San Pedro de Atacama

He was as efficient getting away from Calama, a single terminal pueblo of an airport standing alone in the colorful high
plateau desert serving several daily flights, as he was in battle
with the sun's prowess to descend the horizon before he could
arrive in his new village an hour away, and still have time for
a walk-around before dark. He drove and recalled a tantalizing bit of history from his research that San Pedro de Atacama was originally part of neighboring Bolivia, until a small
military engagement of Chileans attacked to claim ownership,
which included the biggest prize, that being the regions copper
mines. The Bolivians were defeated and the new border was
redrawn just a half hour outside San Pedro de Atacama, which
is still a souring issue with the local Bolivians.

Koda slid open the heavy wooden privacy gate on wheels
belonging to Casa Solcos Boutique B&B and found ample

parking for his rental car, wandered the compound until finding a clerk washing dishes in the kitchen, checked in and grabbed a local map from the front desk. His position was on the southern outskirts of town, and with an easy stroll would be twelve to fifteen minutes from the town center. He had not seen a paved road since exiting Highway 23 and entering San Pedro de Atacama and he would not see another while in town, only dirt; it resembles and remains a village from a time long ago. He also quickly noticed, while he walked nearer to the town center, that the tourist section was generally traffic free. The wind burst up and sand hit into his face, as it will every day in this village. He would eat llama steak for dinner, that being his first time, and he would negotiate a price for a watercolor painting with a local artist, and he would call that day a triumphant event.

Of the many tourists wondering along the main street cutting through the center of San Pedro this morning, probably looking for breakfast before arriving for their excursions out into the desert, none of them would know the incredible accomplishments of Brielle Pierce as she passed them by on her way to work. She was a champion and in her youth, and her pictures adorned several magazine covers. This morning she gathered her latte at El Nortino, where not even the owner, who had made coffee for Brielle for much of the past two years, knew that she was a Biathlete who had once competed in the inaugural coed Biathlon Nationals in her home country of France.

The childhood Brielle was an enigma to her parents as she relished the opportunity to not only jump off a high bridge into Lake Annecy, an act that gave most teenagers pause for a second thought, but she would leap into a double summersault. Adrenaline ran extra thick through Brielle's body as natural as breathing or water does. She was then blessed with a neighborhood boy that also craved competing and living in lock-step with whatever wild notion that Brielle had on her mind. Often Brielle's parents would find him sitting at their table for dinner or without the common sense that he just couldn't slumber over in her bed.

They were inseparable kids. They were track athletes in high school together, whereas Brielle was the only girl racing against boys, and together their formula was consistent; they would seize the lead and throughout both seasons on the track team they would never relinquish, and with him always drafting in the front and carrying his best friend along until the predicable finish when he would coast for the brief second needed, which gave Brielle the time to pass and take the victory and the accolades, as he settled for second place and the trust built between them. Their names and records hang behind a glass case at Lycee Berthollet School still today.

It would be amiss to believe that their endeavors were perfect, as once during their second season there was a minor strife between them and nobody was certain he would take his customary pause allowing her to pass. Perhaps she had boasted earlier in the day that her victories were certain with or without him. Not until he was approaching the starting line had he made his decision. Loyalty between the two would be restored after he won and immediately left the field and walked home without her.

They were both twenty-three years old and competing in Biathlon together on a national level when Brielle first became a darling of the media. It was also the first year that the ski federation allowed women to race against men and at the longer duration of 20 km. It was a bitter cold winter-solstice afternoon in the Alps when the two life-long aficionados had entered the fourth and final shooting stage, and to this point they had played it coy, presenting an image that they might be exhausted, there were five other biathletes in their lead group, four men and one woman, that they had not shaken loose. The two lifelong friends had taken their lanes and harnessed their rifles and the cameras honed in close on them as they breathed in unison and prepared to focus on the target. One final deeper breath and their heartrates were now under control. Brielle would also shoot first by design, as he knew if he shot first she could feel rushed and the consequences and fault of a miss would lie with him. They both hit all five targets and skied back on course joining the other leaders minus one man who had missed two of his targets. This would be the final lap and their synchronized minds had already decided exactly where they would make their push and let everyone else be marionettes of their power. It happened at the base of a long incline the moment he yelled her name back over his shoulder and Brielle responded with a calculated and impatient, "Go," that they accelerated and it was at that moment when Brielle was surging at a sprint past the only other female that the dramatic picture was taken that would cover the magazine the following day with the anguish and panic of the other woman being passed uphill by a smiling, determined Brielle. At the crest they were alone and gone. The few moments that followed were camera close ups that caught Brielle signing to him while he led them into the quiet forest, for she had learned years before that her signing made him calm and faster as he set a pace making the final outcome somewhat predicable. To any spectator analyzing their technique it would be obvious that both having very long legs gave them an advantage of inches with every stride. They were two young people with stories yet to be told and now making their mark on a frozen layer of ice as the camera lost them in the lonely distance meadow with their breathing so intense that it looked like steam blowing from their nostrils. The final excerpt shown that evening was not their interview highlighting their ensconced nature with each other, nor was it him switching tracks before the finish allowing her to be the winner, but rather the two dancing together at the finish area while other competitors lay sprawled on the snow in agony.

Brielle was in her mid-twenties when she first pitched him her fascination with the 24 hour Le Mans car race held every year in western France, and her desire to have them co-drive together. Her attraction centered on the endurance needed to win, as it's who can go the furthest distance within 24 hours that captures the victory. She also imagined a French victory in purity with a French made car, as nothing French had been on the podium in any recent years giving way to Italian, German and English manufacturers. Her novel idea would not be just a French car but a joint venture of two French manufacturers, Renault and Peugeot, assembling the best of what each had to offer, a Renault engine with a Peugeot chassis, creating a symbol of French pride and a shared patriotism, although it would be a onetime experiment whether it was success for bust. The stakeholders agreed to assemble their engineers for an exploratory discussion, which would hopefully lead to design prototypes being drawn up. There was initial progress, and Brielle convinced them to set her out on two weeks of intense training runs to demonstrate her racing skills, to herself and them, and her raw talent was evident in her first run, but her only run, because the project collapsed and closed that week due to budget worries.

Brielle had been friends with two of the police officers in her home town and not the police chief withstanding, who had an enduring fondness for her and an understanding of her adrenaline thrilled addictions, which to this point had always been satisfied with legal activities, but a private arrangement was made between them to push that beyond the boundaries. On a late summer night, actually 3am, a long section of freeway and the on ramps were closed and blocked by the police in Annecy, France so that Brielle could race her motorcycle at a reckless speed down the center lane for just over seven miles. By the time she released the throttle and began downshifting she was no longer thirsty for more speed, contrary, her ethos felt empty and she was ready to discover something purposely benevolent to guide her further. Her lifelong friend had not taken well to success or fame and was basking in the lost comforts shared with a heroin needle. She had taken him to a cabin in the mountains for a forced detox, it did not stick, and he was as cantankerous as a thirsty Black Rhino around the last watering hole. Her mind and heart sought sunnier days in a faraway place.

Brielle sipped her latte and exited from El Nortino aware in her mind that there was a high likelihood that the Director of Parks would cancel all of today's excursions, as he always does when it's extremely windy. The favorite and top-selling trip was several hours of hiking through Valle de la Luna and taking in the glorious desert colors, all bundled up for $65 and just fifteen minutes west of town. If cancelations were coming it would happen just before 10am when all the mini buses were ready to load and drive out. Brielle walked the streets of San

Pedro a cheerful but humbled legacy of her youth, her stride was elegant, no self-preening needed as she was a natural wonder, freckles and all. She unlocked the door of Cosmo Andino Expediciones centered just off the main square and sat behind the only desk to occupy this tourist office, where she was manager and the only employee.

Using a mountain bike offered from his hotel, Koda's agenda was to survey the morning crowd and sign up for an afternoon tour into the desert. He'd peddle a longer route into town taking side streets and gathering data in an effort to satisfy his mind that he had adequate knowledge of this village and could soon give advice to other tourists. Nearly everything was adobe walled, churches from the 15th century built shortly after the Spanish conquistadores conquered the local Incas, dive restaurants and a couple upscale, two night clubs, many hotels with a pool, countless hostels, sandboarding shops, tumbleweed and dust; he was taking it all in. San Pedro de Atacama was built in the 12th century and now he was forever part of it. He circled inward towards the town square, crowds big enough that he dismounted to continue on foot. He entered Cosmo Andino Expediciones where he found Brielle working alone. It was 9:50am.

Do you have a tour to Valle de la Luna? He asked.

"No, I'm sorry, everything is canceled."

There was ample time and reason to induce this meeting into a sensual soiree. They made plans to meet later in the evening whereas she would take him into the desert for stargazing at the international astronomy facility. She had her own keys.

It was a new moon and ideal for finding astrological surprises through the big telescope. They had driven the company tour bus and arrived at the complex around 9 pm. Brielle had brought a blanket to keep warm, and Koda contributed with wine and chocolate granola bars from his travel stash.

The new moon was also ideal for stealth activities. Sergeant Major Gonzalo Lechin de Sucre had been stuck in his position without promotion for years, so he had recently devised a plan to seize land as a gift back for Bolivia and in return his rank would surely be elevated. He prepared Operation Ataque a la Luna, unknown to his superiors, and he would execute in the memory of his great grandfather, who had lost the same ancestral territory that he intended to reclaim. He assembled several fighters consisting of two second lieutenants and the balance were privates, including the youngest soldier of the squadron, his only son Sebastian. Sergeant Major had quarantined his small army off base at a two week survival training to keep them occupied while he wrapped up the details, and to prevent any leaks outside his strike force. His Bolivian fighters carried Glock 17 handguns, Beretta 92F handguns, grenades, Kalashnikov AK-47's and enough ammunition for a three day beat-down. The caravan would consist of five transport vehicles, all Jeeps. Once they were alone out in the salt flats, he halted his troops to explain their mission. He ranted and harangued about the worst injustice ever played upon their country in a speech that was motivationally seditious and at its conclusion he had all sixteen eager combatants in his servitude. The headlights of the Jeeps cast far into the desert as the foray was now real. They drove further through the sand and into Chile, where they caught the 27 roadway east of San Pedro de Atacama.

As later tried in absentia by the prosecutor in La Paz, the Sergeant Major's intent was to seize control of San Pedro's police and local government as a demonstration to La Paz and encouragement to negotiate its forfeiture from Chile.

Brielle and Koda gazed into the core of the Milky Way through various telescopes and also found each of Jupiter's four moons, but for Koda is was seeing the Southern Cross that most peaked his sense of travel. Brielle had learned that back home in Ketchum, Idaho, he operated an extreme mountain climbing service, that he occasionally ran in trail races, and that he had horses on his small ranch. For Koda, he had created three drawers and placed a piece of her into each; one filled with her reserved sweet femininity, one for her simple subtleness, and finally intelligence. He had her figured out. It was midnight when they returned to San Pedro.

For the past two evenings the Chelacabur had not been allowed to open, as penalty by the police for being too loud late into the night. It was a restaurant by day and the tourist favorite night club after the sunset. The Chelacabur was now open and in full volume when Koda and Brielle arrived.

Just shy of 1 am the Bolivians stopped atop a hill on the northeast perimeter of San Pedro. Sergeant Major wanted a final look through his binoculars. The scant streetlights were tired and dim for a village nestled in bed and in need of a greater budget. He was just too far away to hear the music coming from the center of town, and his final order was for Sebastian to remain in a Jeep at this hill for surveillance and back-up radio coordinator. He was only to break silence if he saw any police cars on the move. The four other Jeeps fanned out and pressed into town, where on the north side of the main square; two Bolivian soldiers ran inside the police station and immediately shot the life from the only two officers on duty.

Their bodies teased each other with a harmonious circle of hip movement and sensual touch, and if ever there was a sadness or jealousy in the lives of Brielle or Koda it was lost during this dance as everything exciting and passionate was revealed directly in front of them, and at the moment of crescendo, one Bolivian soldier entered Chelacabur. It would later be noted by a witness, "the cover band was playing a lot of songs by Shaggy when the gunman entered and shot two times at the ceiling. It happened so fast and we didn't know what to do."

Brielle and Koda both wanted to live. They wanted to survive, and to follow orders or lose their freedom would send their brainwaves into a scramble of anxiety. While others froze they had not paused at the moment of terror. Their instincts sent them running out the back door in revolt and to buy the seconds needed to react in self-preservation, and where Koda attacked the soldier caught off guard outside the back door with a direct punch to his throat followed by a kicking sweep to his legs. The soldier was down and his rifle had dislodged from his person when Brielle and Koda both grabbed for the gun. The moment of dominance and skill was upon them as they locked stares into each other. Brielle had a confidence that this was a situation she was built for and he relinquished control of the rifle as the beaten soldier reached for the pistol at his side. Brielle loved her life and ended his. Chelacabur was still in a lockdown of controlled and quiet misery when they both bolted behind a hostel to regroup. They heard either a bomb or grenade detonate, maybe a block away, awaking a disturbed mass of dogs and then another fulminate with such magnitude that a dusty rubble landed on their heads. They moved towards the police station now 200 meters away where they found one of the Jeeps seemingly abandoned and well stashed with guns. Koda urgently outfitted himself with an AK-47 and a sweaty hand full of ammunition while Brielle carried away two grenades into the darkness. The two started northward in the direction of the Meteorite Museum, as it would certainly be a poorly lit area, when they saw three soldiers running at them. Koda's second contribution of the night, after both of them lay out onto the dirt road, was to help shoot dead the oncoming soldiers. No emotion better than panic had yet settled in and Brielle wondered how extensive was this madness and what next to calculate. Maybe if they survived, it would be a discussion as to why they both simultaneously laid onto the ground as those three ran at them. Their instincts alerted them to defuse their attackers with a quick act of submissiveness. They regathered themselves and agreed to walk east on Las Parinas in the direction to her apartment using opposite sides of the street. They had the choice to lay down their guns and walk away under the camouflage of tourists or to trust in themselves and press on. They were cautiously moving east when they saw movement from two soldiers positioning themselves on a rooftop. Koda shot over her head killing one and she shot the other during his brief moment of confusion.

Brielle whispered, "Six."

There was a session of rapid bullets from a soldier into metal, the power transformer was hit and the village immediately went dark. Some radios had gone silent or weren't being answered. The Sergeant Major had not expected or planned for a resistance.

Brielle and Koda scurried to another street stopping to look behind. They were not followed. Between themselves and voices a block away stood an abode wall with shards of glass pressed into the mortar on top as security for the Supermercado. The voices were of Sergeant Major and two soldiers preparing to relocate their position elsewhere in town, but when they started their Jeep, Brielle lobed one grenade over the wall followed by one more tossed over by Koda. The concussion gave them a moment of weightlessness as they were lifted off the ground as debris reached them both and something burnt glanced Brielle in her face. They took the opportunity to run past the Jeep for she knew of a vantage point she wanted to reach. She turned for that curious second to see the destruction they were leaving behind, "Nine," she whispered, not knowing that the handcuffed mayor Morales was strewed to pieces in the back of the Jeep. Brielle used her code on the keypad to enter Stargazing Spa, a code previously shared by the owner and friend, and where she took Koda upstairs, and where they might get to hideout for a couple of hours and wait for help, but in the meantime, if they dared to, they could look out onto the village where they had the vantage of seeing down three streets. She told Koda that just a few days ago she was hot tubbing right here while watching comets race through the sky.

Koda finally asked, "Who are these guys?"

She did not know. She realized that she had never before seen a military Jeep or a soldier in San Pedro. They found water and sodas downstairs at the mini bar and drank-away back upstairs where they felt safer. For ninety minutes Koda would rethink the different scenarios and possible hiding spots if they heard an ambush from downstairs.

The bartender at Chelacabur, Steve Peterson from South Africa with a Work Visa, would later boast to the investigative police how he doused as much area as he could with two full bottles of rum and lit an enormous blaze of fire as a distraction to the soldier still holding them captive. In the shuffle to regain control, the soldier again shot through the ceiling before retreating out into the street and radioing for needed help.

The streets to the west of Brielle and Koda became a flood of screaming tourists in a panic to run for shelter. They had broken free from Chelacabur. The combatant soldier that once held so many tourists in terror was now fleeing without hostage eastward towards three comrades racing to him in their Jeep. The Jeep would roll aimlessly onto a sidewall into a smoky finish as Brielle and Koda emptied half of what's left to the ammo into the three soldiers before adjusting their aim onto the four of what was keeping them from a good night sleep.

It was more than a whisper, "Thirteen."

One eye witness, a local shop owner named Tomas Soto, peeking through his bedroom window would later be quoted, "They are here to rape or to torture or to pillage, I was not certain, but at the moment I found all that was dear to me, my wife."

A chance to catch their breath and ponder if they had done enough to stay free was interrupted by gunfire three blocks away, and followed by an explosion in the direct pathway of reaching Brielle's apartment. Koda suggested that they wear two of the dead soldier's jackets and hats and drive right out of town in one of the Jeeps. "What Jeep?" she asked. The faintest of yellows and grays were touching the eastern horizon that would soon destroy their cover of darkness.

It happened out front of Backpacker's Hostel. A gathering of tourists was growing inside the lobby of folk's frantically calling whomever on their cell phones as Brielle and Koda thought to join them. The yelling of three soldiers was undoubtedly coming their direction and Koda nodded at Brielle that he would be taking his position on a blind corner to the attackers. What balance of physical constitution that remained within him allowed a thrust into an all-or-nothing skirmish when the Jeep turned into his vision and he ended it with the last of his ammo claiming two head shots. Brielle had taken out the driver with a gory borage of eight splattering bullets.

"Sixteen," she claimed.

His AK-47 was now useless to him, so he leaned it against a wall and the two made it to a near sprint of four blocks needed to reach her apartment, where she grabbed her passport and stuffed fresh clothes and such into a bag. Koda found it odd to be standing in this woman's personal world. Maybe the items he had placed into those three drawers were not amble of this incredible person.

The sun and the wind had risen. They walked south, he carrying her bag and she the gun that had become a confident extension of her being. It was she that saw it first, a Jeep parked under a tree with another soldier sitting at the driver's position and facing away from them. She ran at an angry sprint upon his backside catching him without alert as she braced to a stop like a kid sliding into second base with dust canvasing until the referee could make a call. If ten feet is a close range kill then so be it, and with the last of any rage pouring out she mercilessly ended Sebastian.

When they arrived at Koda's room she undressed and starting a refreshing shower to remove the blood spots from her face. Koda joined her as they throttled down from the choke-hold of disparity; the conquer and the surrender had begun. They would afford themselves a rewarding and bonding sex that would reset them onto the luscious side of humanity, and with the transfers of inner rapture complete they collapsed to the pillow for a rest inside the cocoon of ecstasy.

It was 10:45am when Koda gingerly slid open the gate at Casa Solcos Boutique B&B to peek up and down the sunbaked Antonio Leon dirt road and their pipeline out of here. The surroundings to him appeared to be a stagnant and silent coma of fear. Without pushing down on the gas pedal, he simply allowed the car to ease forward through the parkway listening to a sound like popcorn as his tires rolled over the gravel. In her haste to pack a bag, Brielle had forgotten a top and was now wearing one of his T shirts, and he liked that. They took one picture of each other, capturing the moment, that moment of bloodshed now past, but stoic as they remained their lives were not yet certainly free. Koda drove them slowly away avoiding the heart of the village and catching the 23 over the long ago dried up Rio San Pedro riverbed.

The two had made it beyond halfway to the airport when they stopped to use a hilltop on the highway as a lookout for anything disturbing coming at them. They could easily see details for several miles of roadway and waited long enough for a full analysis. There was one car and a minute later another, and it was agreed between them as nonthreatening. It wasn't thirty seconds later when they first caught sight of what they expected; the blue light special was racing their way, a caravan of fresh police that would swallow up and capture everything leaving San Pedro de Atacama. Koda and Brielle positioned their car behind a large rock mound and waited for them to pass, because as they knew, they needed to penetrate any blockade and scathe through unquestioned and without being detained all the way to the airport.

As would later be analyzed on the airport surveillance, Brielle returned his rental car without waiting for a receipt, she only handed them the keys and said that she was late for her flight. Koda was seen studying the departure board where Brielle joined him. They paced the terminal for three minutes before finding the correct counter and where he purchased two tickets.

About the time when the authorities were driving into a chaotic San Pedro de Atacama, was when LATAM Airlines flight 083 was lifting off from the runway. Brielle and Koda were in route and hoping to touchdown in Caracas, Venezuela before being identified.

Two days earlier while Brielle and Koda were first meeting, nine Japanese girls playing in an Under 15 Youth Volleyball Tournament in Caracas were abducted by the El Coqui gang along with their trainers and coach. The Japanese team had defeated Brazil 3-0 and was in transport by bus back to their hotel when they were intercepted by the armed gang and re-routed off course.

Their Uber driver felt a responsibility to update Brielle and Koda of the kidnapping events as reason why his city was in a subdued and nervous state of tension. The gang's financial demands had not been satisfied and the terror was expected to escalate.

Enzo was sixteen days away from clearing out his belongings and retiring from the French Embassy, when at 4:45pm he greeted Brielle and Koda up in his office. He was at that time, Monsieur Enzo Gagne, the Executive Secretary to Ambassador Nadal. Enzo was a man to display his accolades, trophies, plaques, certificates, awards, little statues he brought in from other countries and photos with dignitaries; his office was a mini oasis of a museum.

Koda was only following the tempo of Brielle's explanation as to their survival, as he understood no French, so he wasn't clear on her story. She appeared to him to be vivacious and forthcoming in her speech to Enzo, but there was a dismissive and unpleasant tone in return, and he seemed to doubt the veracity of her story and was bothered further that he might have to investigate this into his evening.

It was Koda who had insisted that they go to the French before his own embassy because he felt a duty to help her first and save her from wrongful prosecution; none the less, they both felt a need to tell their story as a means to prove to each other that they were both innocent.

Enzo was wagging his finger at Brielle and used the corner of her passport to dial his phone.

Brielle whispered to Koda, "He's calling the French Embassy in Santiago to collaborate my story."

Koda would later claim that he expected too much from authorities in that he was actually expecting the embassy to comp their hotel and a flight out. He thought of Enzo as an imperious little man and regretted the mistake of coming here.

Brielle leaned into his ear again, 'They don't have any reports of what we did, and he thinks we are hoaxers."

Koda had been taking stock of the office when he saw a piece that is most unusual. The piece doesn't make sense to his eyes, it's organic and doesn't fit with the rest of the memorabilia. He's mesmerized and counts to himself 11, 12, and 13 notches, he sees the colors, and his mind is triggered to the tales from his two uncles. Could it be? he wonders.

Koda is half American Indian from the Nisqually tribe and was told the tales of such a long colorful bone with thirteen notches and two carvings that went missing from Alaska. Koda has already decided to somehow turn it over and if there are two carvings on the back side then it was the Oosik and he would have to take it with him.

Enzo hung up the phone and told Brielle that she would need to stay at the embassy overnight for further questioning and processing, and then he left his office to initiate some order or inconvenience unknown to them. Brielle watched Koda stick the Oosik into his travel bag and lay his jacket over the section that stuck out.

"I will see you in the morning," he said to her and walked out.

Koda took a room on the 7th floor of Hotel Sabana and tried to get some sleep, but barking dogs along with the possibilities of what the Oosik would mean to his family were both keeping him stirring in bed. He thought that watching news on television would place him into a calm sleep, but reports of routine shortages and routine crime weren't helping, and the story of the Secuestrados Japanese volleyball team with pictures of the nine girls just upset him. He took two pictures of the Oosik and texted it to his older sister, Nancy May, who to his knowledge was somewhere on vacation in Asia or Europe making music. His text would remind her of the tales from the two uncles and in a following text he added, "I could be in trouble, not sure."

IV

Eight people came together on the large deck of Amante Narikala hotel overlooking the city of Tbilisi on a sunshiny afternoon on what became the episode of cocktails with rhymes. Claudia was there to worry further about her farm, Nancy was showing off her new Dado, who himself had brought along his buddy GT Diamond Cutz, who was a local musician and emerging rapper in the hip hop industry.

It was billed as a gathering of strangers to sip cold cocktails on a hot day and bonding as friends, but GT Diamond Cutz was so pissed off that a fellow rapper was recently arrested while leaving his apartment and shown live on TV just 24 hours later in court on charges of using his music to criticize the government and using his music to promote the use of Ecstasy, both of which were false according to GT Diamond Cutz, who easily omitted the known fact that the accused was also a major dealer of Ecstasy pills, regardless, GT was anxious to capture some headlines and reclaim some relevance for the local rap community, so only after GT had all his burdensome irritations out on the table could he then offer himself as a friend.

The third round of cocktails was served and the idea of an outdoor music festival had surfaced. Dado and Nancy would kiss and do that short stare into each other's eyes, and Claudia had offered up her farmland as a venue, and she believed that three or four thousand could easily fit. GT Diamond Cutz said he had all the sound equipment and could put a stage right on top of Claudia's little treasure hole, and he could easily get five or six bands to join in, and that he had radio connections to promote this whole thing.

It was Peter that suggested, "Let's fuse rap with opera." Peter would later say that he was just looking for a new challenge and thought this idea would satisfy the eclectic group at the table. That idea quickly took root, first with GT who had the inner-city slang in his pocket, and with Catherine who relished in the idea of performing opera on stage again.

They selected a Mozart opera about all women being cheaters, there's no such thing as a faithful woman, and all woman will surrender to temptation, and then add in all the men who will bet each other that they can trick each other's girlfriends and thus prove they are cheaters, and you have Cosi fan tutte, which is Mozart's least popular opera.

One more round of cocktails and the
first rap bars were written:

My ho would not pull my weasel
She knows about comin' down lethal
We keep the nooky all nice and equal
Guaranteed that hose queen not nuttin' more people

My brodie speak that my ole lady will cheat
She'll double dip with nothin' discreet
He wants to bet his left nut that backseat dirty in his Ford
They will suck pump and lollipop his pork sword

We blew a little yayo and I heard his term
He'd take my swamp-donkey to 4th base and squirm
On that he doubled or nothing a bag of sand
I'd watch 'em hunka chunka to understand first hand

Joan continues on violin into operatic Catherine who feels abandoned and lonely for her man with verses pulled from Mozart:

This morning I feel in the mood
For some mischief: I've a fire,
A tingling in my veins.
I feel something new
Stirring within me: I'd swear
But why on earth does my lover

Delay in coming?
O heaven! What harm has befallen him?

Describing cheating woman came easy for Peter using his ex-wife as inspiration, but the fun of the day for Peter truly came while watching grown woman sip cocktails and talk over each other with bars and flows about raunchy sex as if everything possible had already happened to them.

Nancy's drums would be needed for both the rap and the opera, unless GT used a drum machine, Peter had the trumpet, and it was agreed that they would buy a clarinet for Leslie to complete everything they needed for an opera.

One more round of cocktails and the next bars about a man trying to get his buddy's girlfriend to cheat were written:

He got in her yard and tried a tongue-jack
She pushed him back a plan outta whack
I'm countin' you were jizz in my pants
Give me a jelly bracelet and pop this trance

Its booty call time and we need an icebreaker
Let's start with your food box 'cause I'm a money maker
Please squeeze my wand of life no need to be a troublemaker
Steeping out deep nibbling my aardvark chaser a cocktail shaker

Dado has enquired of Claudia if he could survey the treasures that she had unearthed, which she accepted with enthusiasm as he told her that he was in a position to purchase the relics if she could keep the whole discovery a secret. Nancy was fine with his arm wrapped around her waist until his alcohol-loosed lips reveal that he's a man with many foreign connections who will trade with any temple, church, synagogue, mosque, or anyone with a phone that needs a new story, and in fact, he's been banned from several digs and chased off from others. The unraveling of these unscrupulous facts got him an unexpected look of disgust from Nancy, and he quickly shook his head and told her that he's only kidding around.

Nancy, wanting to ignore him for a moment was increasingly curious about the text message from her brother Koda and did a quick web search for "Stolen Bone Relics" and up popped Missing Finger of St. Thomas, bone from St. Anthony, and third down was The Oosik with its corresponding article covering the heist of evidence from the police station in Sioux Falls, South Dakota, dated January 2, 1937. Nancy shared the story of Opal's Oosik with her traveling companions before forwarding the article onto Koda with the message, "This is exactly what you have."

V

As Koda would later recall, "I couldn't sleep, so I left my room and wandered aimlessly into the darkness walking north from the hotel." He came upon a historical section of town that may have been popular with the tourists at a time before the civil unrest. He walked alleys feeling guarded against anyone unfamiliar; he was daring someone to screw with him, and he wanted his clear head to return and his bad voices out and he wanted to be home and most of all he wanted to be still. He had unknowingly stumbled into a No Go zone for outsiders. He would say, "I felt like a tracker that was being pulled into certain directions, so I wasn't thinking about where I was going. There was an alley with a door partially ajar and a faint light emitting from inside from what I believed at one time could have been a diner, and it was tantalizing and insisting for a look." He found the girls staged in a back corner lying on a blanket in silence and guarded by one guy sitting on a sofa and seemingly unarmed. Koda snuck up from behind as close as he could before rushing him, and the Oosik will strike him on the left temple with such great force that even the girls knew he was out. Koda chose Aika, who he surmised by her impelling appearance to be dominate of the team and asked, "Are you from Japan?"

"Yes."

"Are there others?"

"No, they took them away."

Koda walked the nine girls single file through alleys two blocks away and hunkered in a hidden area where he remembers that they stood near the base of a statue. He group texted five friends all back in the States, "Urgent. Call the Japanese

Embassy in Caracas NOW. I have nine of their girls. We are on our way. Don't telephone me," and he placed his phone on mute. His app said 11 minutes to destination. He moved them forward, and they passed through a park of mango trees, through Plaza Bolivar; he noticed that they girls were identically dressed in their sports jackets and were all barefoot. He saw two armed men surveying the streets ahead and he lead the team into another dark area. There was no way for him to know if they were gangs or military as they each used similar equipment. Koda found the girls incredibly attentive and obedient to his details of orchestrating their way to safety, so he gave no concern to lead them a longer route and bypassing the two men, they passed a hollowed shell of what was once a TGI Friday's and walked like a mother leading her ducks past the entrance to a tennis club. He led them through one last alley which led onto Avenida Mendoza, three lanes for traffic going north, fifty feet of dirt with large Ficus trees, then three lanes for traffic going south; they needed to cross all of that if they wanted to reach the back side of the Japanese embassy. There were no cars being driven, there were no other people visible at this late hour, except one armed man who was stationed two-hundred yards away north on the street corner, and he had been assigned by El Coqui to monitor anyone attempting to reach the embassy.

On the dark east side of the embassy a bulletproof metal gate was opened and fifteen unarmed strongmen gathered in group. A short flash of light was beamed across the Avenida to where Koda and the girls were waiting, and he flashed his phone light back using a fraction of a second so that El Coqui wouldn't alert to their positon. He placed the girls like they were at the starting line of a race and pointed out the street curbs that they could trip over. He himself was pumping up his adrenaline, as he knew each girl would need to use their own speed and accuracy to reach the other side, and he tells them, "Run like your life depends on it because it does. Don't scream if you fall. I will be right behind you." He selected Sumiye as the girl he figured to be the slowest and positioned himself to follow behind her. He took a deep breath and gave a demanding, "Go."

Koda and the Oosik sprinted to keep up with the girls and as a group they were as quiet as hummingbirds, and every second that he hadn't heard gunfire allowed him to calculate the percentage upward to success. He thought of their parents and he wondered if he would ever meet them. He watched nine girls seeking life with determination and courage that would have made those parents proud. There was no falter and not a step in the wrong direction; it was Haia, their best spiker, who first launched herself airborne and slammed with a thud into the chest of a strongman, eight more airborne and thuds would follow, and Koda reaching the gate abruptly turned south to disappear.

Koda tapped the Oosik onto his skin against his backbone, passed through airport security's X-ray, and boarded an early morning flight for Panama.

That same morning was when Enzo saw that his carved bone is missing and telephoned the U.S Embassy a couple of blocks away. He stated that he had purchased the important relic from an auction in Paris and that he wanted it back.

The truth however was that the Oosik started its journey south to Venezuela nine years earlier when a twelve year old from Mexico named Angel Diaz sat atop the international border wall and pulled his bicycle up with a rope and then let it down into Arizona. It was a Sunday, and he peddled his way for a mile and a half longer into Kino Springs and further yet to a house where he hid behind the bushes in waiting until the home owners left for church. Angel entered a shed, which he found in their backyard next to the well pump house, and where he rummaged over greasy engine parts and piles of tools, past jars of bolts and boxes of screws and up on a back shelf he found a burlap bag that protected the contents of something inside a meter long.

Angel peddled back through town and climbed, with the taste of burlap clinched in his teeth, over the border wall back into Nogales. It needs to be mentioned that during the golden era of local bullfighting, the 1960's, Americans and Mexicans flocked to Nogales and into Plaza de Toros to enjoy the fights. It is nowadays a worn down arena with weeds growing between the concrete seats and the murals of bullfighters have long since faded. There are no more matadors, no more crowds, no swords; it's a closed and abandoned building. Angel brought the Oosik into the old bullring and hid it up on a shelf inside the announcer's booth, just like he had been instructed to do from the very top.

At the very top of those trickle down instructions was Francisco Medina, who was nearing his release after having served five years in Mexico's Islas Federal Prison.

Francisco had used his five years to study the Bible well enough that he could recite any verse and became a de facto priest to the other inmates, and further through his studies he became a connoisseur of religious relics, which prompted his desire to send little Angel north of the border. He had also, during his reign as master of the prison yard, studied law, specifically contract law, which would all fit nicely as a facade to his machinations planned for after his release. He had most recently been researching the conflicts between Luther and the Pope, and he was particularly entertained to learn that Catholics were once paying money to have their sins and future sins annulled, so he plotted to parlay his leadership skills on the outside as priest and a wine producer, and he chose Catholics to be the easiest pickins.

Francisco was released and he dug up his embezzled wealth, which he had buried in a dirt hole behind the same courthouse where he was convicted, and he would use that money to purchase 30 hectares of land in Zacatecas, a wine region in central Mexico, that included a faltering vineyard with a hacienda large enough for a large family and a building that he would convert into a church and a monastery, and he named St. James.

Francisco retrieved the Oosik from inside that announcer's booth, where he once sat next to his father as a child, and then he went south to take the money from Catholics.

For eight years the Oosik was displayed as one of the focal points of his alter, which was intentionally placed ten feet off the floor and inside a glass reliquary so that a close examination wasn't possible. In fact, Francisco laid the Oosik on a purple and golden silk cloth so many of the details weren't visible. Francisco had started and spread the word that he had personally purchased, while in Spain, one of the femurs of St. James the Greater and that was what his congregation was led to believe lay wrapped with the purple and golden cloth, and only an arm's length away from the statue of Jesus. Francisco had his budding congregation, and the Oosik helped it grow to full capacity.

While Francisco was in prison, he had decided that it wasn't enough to just display a sacred relic, like other churches would, but rather he wanted to share his relic for consumption, so he lied to his congregation with a story that the femur bone of St. James was brought down each harvest, and while naked monks stomped the grapes, they would use the femur bone to stir the fermenting juices, and that's the reason why the femur has such colorful staining. His grape was a red Grenache, and he claimed to his exporters that his wine tasted a little spicy because it was touched by St. John's femur; not only spicy, but it was blessed with the micro remains of St. John, and his motto was elements of biblical history in every sip. He further claimed that only the fermenting wine that was in fact stirred and touched by the femur would earn his label, Special Reserve. Francisco paid a kick-back to all local sommeliers that pushed his brand, and the tale of St. John's femur was quickly ubiquitous throughout the region to both wine lovers and Catholics alike.

The name she had written onto her immigration form was Valeria Vera-Bentancourt, and every Sunday for three years she had stood under the Oosik while her fingers plucked the harp. She was a quiet loner, who rubbed her Rosary in church and was a pottery maker of bowls and vases, and she sent money back home to her parents whenever she could. She didn't like any of the men in the town; none of them were marrying prospects for her, and she didn't much care for Francisco either, as he was the only priest she ever knew that carried a pistol.

She held before her a large blob of clay and an anatomy book, and she started to roll out that clay until she had molded what matched a picture of a femur bone from inside her book. With her ceramic replica formed to perfection, she inscribed her initials into it just like she had done with all her bowls, and painted it and gave it to the kiln, and finally soaked it in a bath of red wine. She intended to take St. John's femur back with her to the church where she was baptized.

On a Wednesday afternoon, Valeria slid out the boxes from the church storage to arrange herself several steps up to the Oosik. She was instantly confused about the two carvings and realized that she was not holding a femur bone, but rather something to her that's unidentifiably odd, something without a spherical ball on the end that would fit into a socket; however, she accepted that it must have importance and completed the switch. She rode off the compound inside a truck carrying a full cargo of wine heading east for the coast. At the port town of Tampico, she and the Oosik boarded a passenger boat that took them through the Gulf then veered south through the Caribbean before preparing to dock during the dark of night in Puerto Cumarebo, Venezuela.

A Customs official at Puerto Cumarebo will report that the boat was sailing without navigational lights, thus the crew and passengers will be given extra scrutiny. The Oosik was seized by Customs, and Valeria was informed that they would hold it for thirty days. The Oosik was taken to the customs warehouse, where Enzo's brother-in-law was supervisor, and he took personal possession, and in return gave it to Enzo in exchange for a favorable position working in the French embassy.

Koda and the Oosik flew from Panama and arrived at his ranch in Idaho late that same night, where he scrubbed away the dried blood which had embedded itself the crevices of the Oosik, and he was uncomforted and irritated that the blood splatter of that thug would forever rest down inside of his drainage pipes. He waited for three chunks of firewood to reach a full burn outside in his pit and pulled over his head the driftwood Indian mask that he had painted as a child, and holding the Oosik in front of himself as an offering, he began what his father and uncles had taught him to be a ceremony in pleasing the spirits. Koda danced around his fire until the Oosik not only felt light in weight but was again connected to its animal spirit. He opened a large map of the world onto his dining table and rested the Oosik so it touched both north and south poles and it would remain there until he had his answer on where to go next.

Koda found and contacted me in the morning through articles published in JARO, Journal of American Rare Objects; a peer-reviewed bi-annual journal devoted to archaeology of early American discoveries, and we agreed that I would investigate the Oosik as a freelance writer, which consequently started my travels to Unalakleet, Alaska, and where I first met Aput the ceremonial director.

VI

The wine residue from inside the pores of the ceramic pot were radiocarbon dated at 8,400 years old, which was 400 years earlier than previously discovered at any other archeological sites. That fact would be shared with Claudia, and with Dado, who would be first on site to convince Claudia that a financial agreement and quick transfer of the relics to his workshop were in her best interest.

While Claudia frantically tried to unscramble the mess in her head for a solution, Nancy and Dado walked out to the site where he relocated the bronze dagger into the rib cage of the skeleton and took pictures of his new fabrication, and while he was cataloging the various relics he told a story to Nancy that he'd been working on for the past two days, "This site was inhabited by a decedent of the Tribe of Archer, being one of the lost tribes of Israel, and specifically this site was the domain where his beautiful daughter lived before being decapitated."

Nancy castigated him with, "You cannot just do that," and "Don't you give a shit about any of this?"

Dado offered her the bronze dagger and said, "I can get you a certificate of authenticity if it helps."

"I don't want to be around you anymore; you are not funny," she told him before leaving the farm and deciding that yet another romance has come to its end.

In the time of the afternoon long-shadows, the land of Claudia, the birthplace of winemaking, was a movement of four-thousand jumping dancers, with GT Diamond Cutz, his turntable and computer, with KR80, stunning the crowd with their seven minute rap opera, which Leslie would sum up afterwards with, "That was one of the most satisfying experiences of my life."

Before the second band came on stage, GT took to the microphone and altered history by announcing that his fellow rapper was innocent of these drug charges and it would all come out in court.

Catherine, Joan, Leslie, Nancy, and Peter were in flight to Portugal the following morning when Claudia and her tractor backfilled the ancient site and began marking the row for her new vines.

Nazare, Portugal

Leslie pulled down the drawstrings opening the curtains of her hotel room this mid-august morning giving her a panoramic view of the ocean as she cast out her usual mumbling request, "I want something weird to happen to me today."

While sending out her request to the universe for an odd phenomenon that would humor her throughout the day, she was unaware of four pertinent circumstances which combined would grant her wish, one being that the highest waves in the world, measurably one-hundred feet, were crashing just off her beach, and many of the most extreme surfers were preparing at that moment to conquer such a beast. The second being that a world record for the highest wave ever surfed, eighty feet, would happen this same afternoon. The third being that a super yacht, now moored in the harbor, which she could see but gave little notice, would be what she would sleep on for the next two nights, and finally the fourth circumstance that would satisfy her need for variety would be the learned knowledge that Portugal was the third country to register Wicca, a form of modern pagan beliefs and customs, as an official religion.

The blossoming of this odd-phenomenon continued with the five at Lighthouse Gin Bar eating a late lunch and Nancy meeting and chatting in search of new insights from various surfers. It was the Australians; usually the easiest to meet, from whom she secured a most promising lead, that the super yacht was in fact theirs, and they were overnighting to the island of

Madiera to worship their ancestors and to swim in the ocean with dolphins. Invites on this journey were given and quickly accepted, and instructions were also given for everyone to find their own personal relic, which absolutely needed to come from nature.

Following the guidelines that if it came from nature then everything was acceptable; Joan selected a green and red colored smooth rock from the beach, Catherine purchased a stone necklace from a woman selling her wares on the sidewalk, Peter collected both a raisin and a crab shell to reserve his choice for later, Nancy found a small piece of burnt wood left over from a beach fire, and she would be told later that her selection had extra energy because it was once touched by a force of nature, and Leslie felt connected to a stem of lavender flower she had plucked from a hillside.

The super yacht headed south with a destination closer to Morocco than where any of its passengers had started their morning, which included beautiful witches wearing white robes, a witch that read tarot, a witch with a crystal ball and another one that read palms; there were also three cats roaming freely, there was a virgin fairy named Serenity who wore large pink colored wings and who was tasked with chronicling the customs and ceremonies for entry into the annals of Wiccan beliefs for others to follow on their journey, and there was Banjo King, who would spearhead the upcoming ceremony as Priest, and finally there was his girlfriend, Willow Taylor, who was also Priestess.

As Banjo would explain to KR80, "This boat is our temple and during this voyage we are creating a new ceremony to communicate with our ancestors through mental channeling of dolphins in order to uncover the date when we will die, so that we can prepare for it, and to learn what form we will become during our reincarnation, you need to know that we are using the dolphins as a conduit to the spirit world." He then looked up at the sky and said, "This ceremony must happen when the moon is Gibbous." Serenity then chronicled that new fact into her book of Wiccan ways.

Banjo then asked of them, "Will you write a chant that we can use during this ceremony? Really, anything goes; use humor if you can."

The five used the sunset and wind in their hair at the bow of that boat to find a freedom of expression that they themselves would want to say to their ancestors when given the chance. They considered setting it to hand drums, flutes, and a flamingo style guitar riff, but finally decided that their last song together wouldn't include any instruments at all, and they simply entitled it Kindred Chant with Dolphins, as it can be found within the annals of Neopaganism.

That same evening, Banjo and Willow, were both at work creating the symbolic meaning from Dolphin sounds like squawks, whistles and clicks with their corresponding spirit philosophy, and then they interpreted the various physical movements such as slapping the water with a fin or flipper as well as turning over onto their backs.

In the morning, it was decided by Banjo that breakfast should be forsaken to allow a sharper passage of energies through the dolphins, and it was so noted by Serenity into the book. In groups of two, they leaped backwards from the boat plunging into the ocean surrounding themselves with seven playful dolphins. Greeting your dolphin would become the new custom, which included waiting for the dolphin to choose you, followed by a short freestyle dance together, and completed with a kiss on the mouth if the dolphin presented itself willing.

This swim with the dolphins was a blissful and yet sorrowful time for the five as they would return to Portugal and commence their flights back home.

The dolphin, which had chosen Joan, was pushing herself under her arm and encouraging her to hold onto the fin for a towing. It was previously agreed that they would not grab onto the dolphin, but this one was insistent, so Joan played along and was whisked away at full speed from the boat further out at sea before releasing herself and swimming back under her own power. It was overlooked by everyone at that time, except Banjo, to the significance of this spirit act.

Rocks were placed in a wide circle around the deck of that boat, a table was placed in the center of the deck where all relics were displayed as if on an altar to absorb the energy from the dolphins, which also included a goat hoof, the larynx from a goat still stuffed inside of a small glass jar, a horned pagan doll, one Viking pendant, and one small mirror.

Banjo wore a helmet with curved horns and Willow wore a floral head wreath. It was time to see where we each go upon death. All standing in a circle holding hands, Willow gave her opening prayer to several gods, and Banjo spoke to the Dolphins. Mediation would follow and then Banjo would read aloud each line from Kindred Chant with Dolphins, and in chorus it was repeated:

Greetings for all people that I know with shared name
Whether long ago shared blood or raptured in memory
I wish to know you and care you're proud just the same
Passing through wise dolphins is my way of extrasensory
Please god and goddesses tell me of what you became
Is thy spirit bug or tree or something more complimentary?
I am ready to hear what happens to me after captivity
Strangled breathless by investors, molesters and protestors
Let us connect Wiccan energy and discover during this festivity
Show me the Otherworld and be silly my cherished ancestors
From womb of my delivery through wisdom of my witchery
This step in my history is to be open as inquisitive requestor
Whether I will be a loud black crow or shiny rainbow or an embryo
I have been blessed with my overabundance of pleasure
What will I be called to do? I am excited to know
I raise my arms to you in a worthwhile measure
Dried leaf falls from its tree with its place the winds decide
Justify me a flower or tree and your praises are glorified
Yes! Yes! The vision you send is nearing through the darkness
With all my energy and excitement I accept the unknowing
I will blurt out what I see passionately and clearly and regardless
Colors have dispersed to my afterlife and now my conscience is overflowing
The solution to my answer is clearly a happy celebration
Now I will say out loud what came through this creation
My vision in the afterlife is ______________.

Joan spoke that her spirit on earth had graduated through all lessons and upon her death her spirit would begin on another planet. Peter said that he had to start over as an earthworm. Catherine saw herself reincarnated as a man. Nancy would reside in limbo as a guardian angel to five children until their duration on earth had passed, and Leslie would be content swimming the ocean for ninety years as a beautiful turtle.

VII

Koda entered the office of the Consulate-General of Japan in downtown Seattle where he explained his desire to "meet and say hello" to any of the nine girls from the volleyball team that would have an interest in seeing him. He would go onto explain that he felt compelled to see their faces and disposition in a manner vastly improved from that moment he left them in terror. He simply needed to know if they were coping and improving from that traumatic episode, and he thought that if they could ensconce on their turf that it would benefit not only them but himself as well. The Consul General agreed to forward Koda's email address onto the families of each girl, and if they desired to meet, then Koda would get a response from them personally.

The following afternoon, Koda and the Oosik cleared Customs in Kyoto, Japan and boarded a train traveling two hours north to Nagiso; a small village town in the mountains and home for two of the girls.

During dinner at his little country-style hotel called Kohsinzuka, Koda listened to the owner tell animated stories of Japanese folklore and traditions until that owner inquired of the Oosik, which Koda had laying at his side. Koda shared his story of the Oosik with the other guests and that owner, and when he described the act of using the Oosik to save the girls he was immediately recognized by the owner as the man with valor that saved his niece, Chinami, whom Koda would be meeting in the morning. Koda listened to the owner tell him how wonderful it was that he had come here to see his niece, and that he was sure that his visit would help with her anxiety.

The hotel literally touches the historic Tsumago to Magoma trail, used for centuries to travel north and south through Japan, and at 9am a girl that Koda did not recognize, Chinami, because he had not seen her before in the daylight, approached him outside his hotel; she was with her father, both ready for a hike with Koda. She placed a necklace with a small bell around his neck and told him that this would scare away the wild bears. Koda carried the Oosik and had already decided not to mention its use unless she recognized it and asked. Chinami told Koda that the hike was six miles and that she preferred to complete it without stopping for a rest. There was little said during the hike, but Koda remembers catching her staring at him with curiosity many times, which comforted him as he assumed she was processing how to trust strangers once again. She had set a quick pace and expected both of the men to not fall behind, when suddenly she abandoned her quest to make it nonstop and turned to request the Oosik be placed into her hands. Both her father and Koda were catching their breath from the pace as she examined the Oosik; she examined the Oosik not for its markings or color, but as a weapon, and she used it to smack it lightly into an open palm to feel the potency of its force.

"I remember you using this," she told Koda and handing it back to him with a smile, and with that smile Koda had everything he wanted from her and the trip was a success no matter what else would happen.

The following morning was a Sunday and Koda went to the house of Mikazuki and ate breakfast with her entire family, five children and both parents are teachers, and the family, including Mikazuki, mostly wanted to understand why Koda was in Venezuela and how he found the volleyball team. Mikazuki hurried through her breakfast in anticipation for the event that followed: rock climbing near their backyard. She was harnessed in and Koda was given the ultimate prize: to be the trusted belayer while their daughter ascended the face of a sheer cliff a little over sixty-feet to climb. Mikazuki climbed with unreserved enthusiasm while Koda anchored himself and focused on paying out the rope for a perfect climb. The oldest sister said to Koda, "She's showing off to you," and Koda took that as a sign of recovery.

His purpose became clearer and it happened during the train ride to the city of Takayama, during which the Oosik was stared at and whispered about by other passengers as if it were a celebrity, Koda actually wondered what would happen to the Oosik if he gave it to someone to hold while he went into the bathroom, that circumstance would not happen he knew, but this is where Koda was able to put the Oosik into perspective as to where he needed to hand it off.

He recalled the history of The Honjo Masamune; a sword that was passed down from one emperor to the next over hundreds of years, it was and would be still a Japanese national treasure, except it was forcedly surrendered to the U.S army at the completion of WWII, it was handed to an unidentified U.S Serviceman and the swords whereabouts are left a mystery. Koda became lost and marveled with the fantasy that he had possession of that sword and was touring Japan on a trip paid for by the Emperor's family because he was traveling north and had prearranged a ceremonial hand-off in which he would be returning the sword to the Emperor, and he imagined further, although several security guards were following his every move, that a great trust had been bestowed on him and that nobody would dare interfere with his journey until he successfully reached Tokyo. It was during the vanity of that fantasy that Koda realized that he needed to return the Oosik to the Inuit people of Alaska, and he texted his sister Nancy of his plans with encouragement for her to be witness during the handoff.

On Monday, Koda and the Oosik were led by the school master into the room where they interrupted English class and met Kiko for the second time. Koda was delighted that a teenager would leave her seat and introduce him to her peers with enthusiasm. The teacher surrendered her duties and allowed Koda to hold conversation with her class. He brought up topics in history and western horseback riding and American girls, and he identified the traits coming from Kiko that she thought of herself as beautiful and necessary, which satisfied his purpose in being there that morning.

At precisely 6 o'clock he made his entrance into the restaurant owned by the parents of Sumiye, where the chef was normally her father, but not for Koda this evening, as Sumiye was taking charge of preparing food for her guest. Koda went straight for the kitchen and found her hunched over slicing tomatoes, and she was the first girl he recognized from that awful evening almost one month earlier, for she was the one that he assumed would run the slowest of the group. For their appetizer she made them Caprese but with a new twist by adding in slices of pear. The two ate dinner and made their peace together that what had happened in Venezuela was terrible but they would wake up every day and smile at the sunrise.

The second and only other girl he recognized was Aiko, and two others whom he didn't remember, Morina and Sakura, all left the dugout to give him a hug before telling their softball team who he was to them. Koda watched their game, he watched their efforts to win, and he felt enriched that his life had intersected with theirs and he felt internally pleased that those three would grow into a career and families just like most everyone else, and he expected to one day be forgotten by them in the hustles of life, but that was alright by him.

Koda with the Oosik sat inside the office of a either a counselor or psychologist, at the time he wasn't sure which title she carried, and this was a first for him to sit with anyone that professionally analyzed depression and nightmares; in fact it was his first visit to a shrink for any reason, and in walked Kaiya with her mother, who was the eighth and final volleyball player to accept his invitation to meet.

Koda told Kaiya, "it is awesome to see you," and he remained optimistic throughout the session; he talked about the activities he likes to do back home, and told her that he too was scared that evening when they met, but he wasn't going to let that man keep him from feeling happy. He suggested to the counselor that they all go for a walk outside because he thought that body movement was a good thing for both Kaiya and himself. They were circling the block when Koda stuck out his hand and she took it into hers. "Let's get some ice cream, my treat," he told them. It was inside the ice cream shop when the counselor told him the fate of their coach and trainers back in Venezuela, about how Kaiya's father was among the three that were hung and burnt on a street inside the No Go zone with their wallet and identification placed below their scorched feet.

Today the Oosik is displayed at the Unalakleet museum alongside the seal skin pouch that once secured the Oosik during its journey with the three daughters of Ujurak.

VIII

It required two helicopters to transport all eleven people to the ceremonial handoff taking place on an ice covered plateau near the summit of Mount Osborn, the highest mountain on the Seward Peninsula and vantage point to the ancient pathway of the Oosik.

It was Tuesday, September 19, 2017 when Koda spread open his thick parka onto the icy ground and gently nestled the Oosik within the fur lining. I watched him touch it for the last time before he stood in separation as a parent would upon releasing their child off to college for the first time.

Nancy took a deep breath of the cold air and blew into a Native American Flute, which is a simple wooden instrument with five finger holes, and projected a beautiful solemn sound that echoed across the mountains. When the echo fell silent she passed the flute onto Leslie who sucked in as much air as her lungs could take and bellowed out a sound of tranquility that echoed, and when it fell silent it was Joan's turn to serenade the Oosik and its passage, and the flute was handed to Catherine who licked her lips and made the sounds that the animal gods were expecting, and finally Peter played every sound that he could get from that flute, like he was fearful to come to a conclusion and not until he felt that his music had touched every glacier did he quit.

The echoes were silent and four decedents from Ujurak the shaman, Inuksuk, Aqakuktuq, Aeeluk, and Tapeesa who was the only female, together lifted up the Oosik, and later that afternoon they returned with it to the burial site of Ujurak.

The End

This book is a work of fiction. Names and
characters are products of the author's imagination
and used fictionally. Any resemblance to actual
persons, living or dead, is entirely coincidental.

ABOUT THE AUTHOR

Scott Nitzel was born in Oregon at the end of 1961. Today, he remains tied to corporate & financial industries as a means to frequently escape as an Earth Explorer, which has allowed him to freely roam throughout seventy-two different countries, then during the summer of 2020 while our world was shut down he extrapolated a copious amount of his thoughts into the writing of this book.

For information please contact Scott Nitzel
sdnitzel@yahoo.com